The Sister and McGuire

Books by Simma Leslie

The School Teacher and McGuire

The Best Man

The Sister and McGuire

SIMMA LESLIE

iUniverse, Inc.
Bloomington

The Sister and McGuire

iUniverse books may be ordered through booksellers or by contacting:

iUniverse
1663 Liberty Drive
Bloomington, IN 47403
www.iuniverse.com
1-800-Authors (1-800-288-4677)

ISBN: 978-1-4620-0645-8 (sc)
ISBN: 978-1-4620-0646-5 (ebk)

Printed in the United States of America

iUniverse rev. date: 04/26/2011

This book is dedicated to my daughters,
Rudya Catherine and Idenne Margaret
I will always love you.

Chapter I

Brad McGuire paced back and forth on the deck of the Delta Queen. The paddle wheel-ship was sailing down the Mississippi to New Orleans from Saint Louis. McGuire's reason for being on this ship was his sister, Helen. He was taking his sister back to New Orleans to live with him. He could not believe that she actually was all that was left of his family or that he would end up responsible for her.

Brad McGuire was well over six feet tall with hair the color of sunshine He had a smile that made many a woman feel it was just for her. His teeth were white and gleamed like pearls. He had a Roman nose that went well with his square jaw and his very bright lake-blue eyes. Brad walked quietly like a panther, silent, but ready to pounce.

He looked off into the distance. He saw the river lapping against the surrounding land of the Mississippi, so desolate and wild. He sure never wanted to be on that forsaken land. He felt lucky to be on the ship, instead of horseback or even worse, on foot in that bleak land. He was blest that he never had to be on the land around the Mississippi. It sure looked like it was full of mud, trees, and of course snakes, bears, and other wild animals. Nothing he was use to in all his long years. He came from the South, and went to the West. Only he knew what he was facing, in the West. At the time he went West, he did not care much about anything.

He had his share of troubles when he fought for the south. He remembered the bleakness he felt as he watched the northerners burn the many plantations. The devastation of the burnt land had struck him like a knife into his heart. The times he went without food as there was none to be had when they were waiting to attack. The South had lost the war. There was no going back to the time of the plantation or of the old South. McGuire knew he was on loose ends not knowing where he was going or what he should do.

He never dreamed that Helen would come back to America. He was so sure she would stay in England after they lost their plantation. She was so pretty, that he was sure she would find an English husband to her liking. She was petite, but so filled with sunshine. She lighted up each place she visited. Why did she leave England so suddenly? There had to be a reason. What had happened? Sad thoughts lodged in Brad's mind. Helen was younger than he was by two years, yet he always knew he was responsible for her. He had to find out the reason she had come back to live with him. Live with him? A gambler, a no good for nothing man! He had to do better by her than he had by himself. He had to find something he was good at so she would be happy. Could anyone be happy with this mess of the North winning the war and out for revenge. Still, when he thought of it, Helen's eyes showed a sadness he could not understand.

In his youth they owned a beautiful plantation, tall stately, with six marble columns. It had bedrooms in the second floor. The slaves that worked in the house lived on the third floor. Downstairs the living room and library gleamed with oak wood. The reception area was covered with ivory silk. Outside the house, the kitchen was run by slaves; the kitchen was safe from fire as it was not connected to the main house. The house gleamed white in the sunshine. Since the war there was nothing left of their plantation and of course of their wealth.

Helen had gone to a live in England with his mother's sister and her husband. Brad's mother was English, but had left England when she married her husband, the owner of the plantation.

It was from what little money Brad McGuire had scrapped together that enabled Helen to make the trip to England. She did not belong to a ravished land of no plantations. She should have silks and satins to cover her body. A royal man to see to her needs. He hoped she would marry a Ton Englishman, rich and well known. Then his worries about his sister would be over. His obligation to his family would be finished. But no, here she was, back with him. Whatever was he suppose to do with her? She was so sad, he could see it in her eyes.

McGuire was a gambler, straight and simple. He was a gambler, because after the war, it was the only trade he desired. He knew how to run a plantation, and gamble like any gentleman of his breeding. Not too long ago he owned a hotel, saloon and whorehouse. He had a wonderful mistress LouLou. He gave that all up. LouLou wanted him to stay but how could he stay? The property he owned was never kept long by him. Just long enough to make it a paying proposition. All that property was given to him by his Uncle. Even though it made lots of money, he gave them away. The war had done something to him. No! It wasn't the war really. He wanted to be free, that is - he had to hide from Samantha and be free from thoughts of her.

Samantha was her holy name. The reason he felt unsettled and alone was because she married someone else. He loved her. He never realized how much until she tuned him down to marry Ted. He could not stay in the same town or territory that she was in. His mind cried out that he would never be holding her slim body next to his. How he longed to feel her warm flesh, and sweet lips against his. He had to leave and yet, the ghost of Samantha followed him wherever he went. He knew he would never be free of her.

Before he could get use to the idea of his loss, his sister, Helen, was coming back to America. No explanation even, no excuses, just she was coming back to live with him. So he went up to Saint Louis to met her. He could do nothing else. He just did not know what he would do with Helen now. Once they got to New Orleans, then what was he to do? What was she going to do? Would she expect him to do something besides gamble? Of course, he was a gentleman, and he had to earn a living, a decent living, that she would approve of.

McGuire lit his cheroot. His red boots were hand tooled and inside the boots there was a place for his Bowie knife. He wore red holsters with his favorite silver guns. His pants were striped, tight fitting black with silver stripes. His coat was black and had tails. His shirt was ruffled and a cravat of silver was tied neatly in place. He had a big diamond stick pin. He dressed as a gambler would. Forgotten was the black outfit he wore with LouLou. He showed he was a gambler by the clothing he wore.

McGuire once thought he would never have to work, that was before the war. They owned the largest plantation in the state. He was bowed down to and kissed by all. Now he just wanted to tumble around the world, just having Lady Luck at his side. Any thing was better if he never thought about Samantha. His life was empty and his mind was filled with what might have been if he had acted differently. Why would Samantha not want him? All the ladies loved him, at least he thought that.

He had won 500 dollars that he put into his pocket. He felt good, at least he won. He won the money in a hard fought battle with other professional gamblers. Now he just wanted some air and to think about what to do about Helen. He saw his sister on deck, some thing he told her not to do. He knew that she would cause trouble if the other men saw her. He just was not up to a duel over her honor. He could not think straight with her on his back. He wanted to think of nothing, and nobody.

"Why did you come back to America?" asked Brad

Helen looked at him with tears in her eyes. She had lost some of the sun shine she always shared with everyone. She looked so miserable.

"Do you want to know? I can't tell you now. It has to wait," said Helen with tears in her eyes.

Brad McGuire nodded his head and turned around. He could not look at her as she stood in front of him with tears in her eyes.

Instead of screaming at her, he looked around the steam boat. The upper deck cabins were box-like superstructures. The tall, twin smoke stacks stood out against the sky. They provided a good draft for those who fired boilers. The Pilot house was on the main deck for longer views of the river.

The ship was long and narrow with a flat bottom. There were no docks to land at, so the bow of the boat would angle into the entry way. The boat rode on the mud and sand of the sloping riverbank. Then when it was close enough to land, it used gangplanks to reach the dry land. To counteract the river current, they would slowly turn the paddlewheels in the opposite direction of the river.

The main decks were higher, and one deck was made wider and longer. But beauty could not be left out, so decorations were added to the superstructure. Ginger bread architecture, and painted wheelhouses, feathered smokestacks and carved decorations on the pilothouses and cabins became the rule.

Brad McGuire kicked the railing around the main deck.

"I told you to stay in your cabin. Why in the world are you out where everyone can see you?" asked Brad

"Brad" came the sweet voice of Helen. "Brad, I had to come out to get fresh air. I am so tired of being locked up."

McGuire turned around and looked at his sister Helen. She was beautiful. In fact, he thought, she is stunning. She should have found a nice Englishman to marry. He could not imagine what he would do with her in New Orleans.

Helen had golden hair, just like McGuire. She had the same Lake-blue eyes he had. She had a little straight nose and a rose bud mouth. Her lower lip was fuller than her upper lip. She looked kissable. What in the world was she doing here? Her face was a perfect oval. She looked and acted as royalty.

She smiled as she rushed to him and kissed his check.

McGuire pulled her close to him and kissed her forehead. "Look Helen, I just don't like the gamblers on this ship. That's why I want you to stay in your cabin. I looked out just a short while ago, and I saw you sneak on deck. You have to listen to me. I told the other people I was playing with I needed a breath of air and would be right back. I want you to stay in your cabin, That's why I stopped gambling. Hey, I was winning. I have all of five hundred dollars to proof it. Don't know if Lady Luck will be back with me when we start gambling again."

"Brad, I don't know why you say that. You live by cards and I guess you will die by cards. You never take anything very seriously. You're a gambler. So what is so wrong? If you can be one, then-"

"Helen, they are not gentlemen like you know. I gamble because, well because there is nothing left to what we had. I can't go home again. But you have a bright future ahead of you. You should have married while you were in England. I can't understand why you came back. Back to what?" Brad McGuire kicked the deck again.

"Oh, Brad, I wanted to be with you." Helen said as she smoothed down her hopped skirt of silver blue without the hoop. It dragged on the floor. It was the old fashion that she wore when there were plantations. She wore a short jacket of silver blue that hugged her slim body. A silk blouse of deep royal blue showed under her short jacket. Her slippers were a royal blue and she carried a blue little parasol. The parasol had ruffles of silver blue. She was not wearing her hat, as she only wanted to sneak on deck to see if she could find her brother. Her loose bun she wore, made her hair blow around her face.

She looked so doll like, and there etched a sad smile on her face.

McGuire huffed and puffed, but he knew it would do no good. Helen was here and there was nothing he could do about it. He looked at his sister. She was petite, a package of sun. She was five foot three, and she was whip thin like the limbs of a new magnolia tree.

"Oh, Hell," McGuire muttered under his breath. He took Helen's arm. "March yourself down to the cabin and stay there. No lip. We are staying right now in New Orleans near Royal Street in a house owned by Annabelle Smithy. We have room and board there, well, at least I had room and board there. I hope she'll take you in. Then we will see what we can do so you- well you know. Maybe we'll leave New Orleans and find something else to do."

Helen stood very tall for her petite statue, and looked at him. "I'll go whatever you say, but please, I am so tired to being cooped up. Let me get some air sometimes soon."

McGuire stopped speaking and looked at his sister He was about to propel her down the steps to her cabin when he heard a splash. He dashed to the rail of the ship and looked over it. He saw a woman trying to stay afloat in the rough flowing waters. He thought she would die in the wind swept, rough waters. Especially as she had that full skirt dragging her down. His compulsion, he had to save her. He didn't even think about why. He pulled off his boots, his coat, his holster. his silver tie, and guns. Maybe he felt boxed in, or something he could not describe.

McGuire yelled to his sister, "Take care of these, and go to the address I just told you. Wait for me there" McGuire jumped up on the railing and dived into the Mississippi River as it boiled over trees and rocks.

Helen stared after her brother. She watched as he reached the woman who was being dragged down by her clothing. She saw McGuire pull her up by her hair. He pulled another knife he always carried out of his waist and cut the woman's clothing. She heard him yell something to the woman but could not make it out. Her heart beat with the knowledge that she was all alone. What was the address he just gave to her? Would she remember it later, as she was not to sure of it now.

The paddle wheel kept churning and the man and woman in the water were left behind. Helen felt tears run down her eyes. She didn't know what she would do if anything happened to her brother. She picked up his boots, guns, gun belt and coat. She cuddled it close to her chest. She knew she was taking a terrible risk by coming to New Orleans when she found out where he was. She could have stayed in England, but it just wasn't her home. At least, she could not stay there because it was Edward's- Oh Edward!

England. She remembered every thing that happened in England and why she came home. Maybe, not real home, but at least near her brother. She walked slowly back to her cabin. She sat on the bed and shook. She had to wait to see what had happened to him. They had just passed Baton Rouge. It won't be long before they were in New Orleans. She could not imagine what she would do without Brad, her brother.

Should she get off the ship? What if he drowned? What was she to do? Tears ran down her checks as she wondered if she had done the right thing in coming back to America. But how could she stay in England? She pulled out her handkerchief and wept into its clean white folds. She did think of her Aunt and Uncle. They would send her money, but what could she do until then? She was stranded.

*　　*　　*

Helen paced her small cabin. She had to get a hold of herself. But--oh but-. England, Edward! She can not forget him. He was so tall, six feet seven inches. He towered over her. He had blond hair, so blond it was almost white, and his eyes were a stormy gray that penetrated into her heart. His funny crooked smile always made her feel so loved. So much for Edward! She heard the ship docked already, and she had to go ashore. She would wait to be the last one to shore. Brad, her brother, had insisted she not cause any fuss.

When she thought of Edward she thought of his mother. A real pain! His mother had wanted him to marry money. Not someone who was penniless like she was. He had said he loved her, but his mother was another matter. He could not stand up against his parents.

She hoped that her brother Brad was all right. He never was the same since he came back from the war. He always took such chances. As if he didn't care if he lived or died. Imagine his jumping into the Mississippi River when he saw the woman going down in the currents. Helen knew he was a strong swimmer, but to take such a chance for someone he didn't even know. She wondered if she had done the right thing by coming to live with Brad. And now, she did not know if Brad was alive or dead.

Helen walked out of her cabin. She had put all of Brad's silver pistols, and clothing into her suitcases. She did not know what else to do with it.

She knew how to shot very well. Brad had made sure of that during the war. To protect yourself, he had insisted. Now, she didn't even know where she was going and what would happen to her. Every thing was all so new and different. Nothing was like what she knew in South Carolina or England. A ship tossed in the sea was better equipped than she was because she was at a lose of what to do. She did not know what to think even. She walked down the plank of the ship, with two sea men carrying her luggage. This was all she had in the world, and Brad, her brother, had not promised her much more.

Helen was the last passenger to leave the ship. She carried her little parasol in one hand, and held on to the gangplank rail going to the shore with her other hand which also held her long dress. She wore a small hat of silver-blue perched on her blond hair that was swept back into a cascade of curls.

She tried to remember Brad's words- Royal Street, Annabelle Smithy. Where was Royal Street? How long was it and how far away? She straightened her shoulders as she walked down the gang plank. So far, everything she did turned into dust. The guns she had packed seemed to lower her resistance to life. Maybe she should have just killed herself? She had nothing to look forward to. What she wanted was her love, and it had turned to dust. She still loved Edward no matter what had happened, but it was so hard to think. All she could remember was her lost love, and nothing seemed real to her. She should never have come back to America. She should have stayed in England or maybe Ireland, but she did not belong here, she knew it. Actually, she did not belong any where in this world. What had she expected? What was real?

She pulled herself together and looked around the wharf. The baggage lay at her feet. She was alone on the wharf, no other carriage was to be seen, except one. It was surely taken by someone of quality. She could see the crown on the door. It blazed in gold relief. She saw it and could not help looking at the carriage.

How strange to see a carriage like royalty. Maybe she was going mad? Or had she lapsed back into England? She took a deep breath and let it out slowly. Her life was a mess and she was so afraid. She closed her eyes and counted to ten and then opened them again. The strange carriage was still there.

Chapter II

Louis LaCount was sitting in his carriage watching the people descend from the ship. He was waiting for Clarese, his mistress, to come out of the ship. He knew he could not keep Clairese, She bored him. Just as he was bored now; he was waiting to see if she was dead. His men would kill her quickly and quietly if she was guilty of having bought a man to kill him. He had her long enough, and now was the time to get rid of her. Usually he would send someone to see if she got off the ship, but he had to know for certain. He had heard she was going to get someone to kill him.. Him! She was crazy to think he did not know her every move. She was going to see her mother she had said. He knew her mother was a woman from New Orleans. A half breed! A woman who would sell anything for a hit of dope. The mother was long dead. It was the grandma that sold Clairese when she was only eighteen years old. The grandma was a liar. Clairese was unbelievably lovely, but she knew nothing of value. He had never seen any one like her before as she had the face of a Madonna . That was when he cleaned her up and claimed her as his. Such a long time ago, but he been a fool to have bought her. What was he thinking at the time. That was why he sent people to watch her and kill her if it was true that she had hired some one to kill

11

him. But if she was on this ship, he would be able to see her face and know if it was true that she hated him enough to kill him.. She might fool the others, but she would not fool him. He knew her too well. She would never expect him here He was beginning to fancy the ways he would kill her.

LaCount was thin as a whip, with skin the color of mahogany. His eyes were green chips of ice and his mouth was a straight line with an unforgiving look. He stood six feet tall but he seemed to tower over every one who came near him. He had a square jaw that made people tremble when they saw him. He had an unforgivable nature.

He did not know why Clarese had said she wanted to see her mother. He did know she had no mother any more. Personally, he wondered why she went and if it was true she wanted to kill him. There was something very strange about her going. That was why he knew in his mind she was a turn coat. Most of all, he wanted to know who she had chosen to kill him. She knew without a doubt, he had found a new love.

His eyes racked the ramp coming off the ship. He saw Helen and something happened to his breathing. She looked like an angel that was floating down from heaven. Her face was the face he dreamed about. The one he knew he would never see in person. He caught his breath. Never had his heart stopped as he stared. He could not believe that his dream was coming true. She was coming down the ramp followed by two sea men. He watched transfixed. His heart thumbed harder in his chest. His breath was caught in his throat as he watched her. He could not believe his eyes. In fact, he would have sworn he had no heart to lose. He knew his limbs were fast becoming ready to jump. He hadn't come this far in New Orleans to have a heart. He was feared by everyone and owned so much property, money and people that no one ever opposed him that is except one person. He hated that white bigot, McGuire. He would kill him one day.

He leaped from his carriage as he watched Helen emerge from the top deck. The door to his coach swung back and forth as his man tried to control its swing. He was transfixed as he stared at her silver billowing skirts as they swayed as she walked. She looked like a queen stepping into her throne room. A person of greatness to have people bow to in respect and love unconditionally. It was him, who loved her unconditionally. He could not believe that he loved her, without even talking to her. He felt his heart beat to the rhyme of her walk. He felt his flesh go weak with the sight of her just walking the gangplank.

He observed Helen McGuire step on shore. He watched her as she looked around the landing. She looked so scared and lost, in spite of her regal air. He knew she was looking for a cab, but they were all taken already. She had waited too long to get a cab. Louis carefully walked slowly towards Helen. As he walked he noticed every detail of her beautiful, thin body Her bosom pressed in gentle curves under her dress. Her fingers were long and thin as they beat against her dress. She had an aristocratic tilt of her head, but her eyes held tears close to the surface. Her pale golden hair flapped with the wind in her face. Her hat titled with the wind. It was about to blow off, he thought.

He walked up to her. She looked up at him. He noticed her lake-blue eyes, which reminded him of someone he hated, McGuire. But McGuire never said he had any relatives. He tipped his black bowler. He was dressed in a black suit jacket, black pants and a purple shirt with a cravat of lavender. He had a large diamond stick pin in his cravat. He saw her eyes look in wonder that a man was wearing such colors. He wanted to laugh. He noticed her eyes looked not only as one lost, but like she carried a well of sadness hidden in its depths. He noticed the little hat perched on top of her golden curls like a bird ready to fly away. Her nose was straight and her checks were high. Her face was a perfect oval. His mistresses might have been prettier than she was, but she was regal and she smelled of old money or at least blue blood. Many of his mistresses were exotic, and would do anything he wanted, but he knew this was different. He had seen an angel and he wanted that angel for his own, forever. He always got what he wanted. There was no excuse for anything different. He had many mistresses in his life, but he wanted this one for always. He felt his heart pounding. He reached out his hand and touched her shoulder.

He felt her flinch. She was not about to let a black man touch her. She shook her head and looked at him in horror. Her mouth made a perfect o. She shook her head and stepped back from his hands.

"How dare you touch me?" she asked in a voice that rose too high.

Louis looked at her and wanted to laugh. This was the lady he was going to have as his wife. A white ghost of the old South. He could smell it in her stance.

He took off his hat and held it in his hand. Than he looked at her with a possessiveness that he owned her. He knew she will welcome his touch, or at least get use to it.

"May I help you? You seem lost." said Louis He held a walking cane that had the face of a dragon engraved on its top. The dragon leered at her. She felt the coils of the dragon around her body. She knew she was prone to thoughts -but this was too much.

Helen looked at him and lowered her eyes. He was a black man. She could not think very straight just at this moment. She wasn't sure of where to or what to do. It was not right to speak to a black man, and to have him touch her was outrageous. He seemed to see right through her and laughed at her antics. She had never met a man that read her mind. Even Edward - but no, no thinking of that. "I was looking for a cab to take me to my brother's room. He has a room, that I hope I can use until-."

"You have a place already?" asked Louis as his eyes bored into her face.

"Yes, it is my brother's, as I just said," said Helen as she twirled her parasol around her feet. She was in a dream world where black people spoke to white women.

"Your brother's? Are you related to Brad McGuire?" asked Louis as he studied her fumbling attempts to look cool. He could feel her fear; it leaked from her body. Her eyes, she had to be related to McGuire, the man he hated with all his heart. Some day he would kill him. Slowly, with much torture.

"Why yes, He is my brother. Do you know him?" Helen smiled and looked up at him. His heart beat so fast, he hardly caught his breath as he watched the smile on Helen's face. Then quickly she looked down again. His eyes bored into her brain. She felt a sudden fear of this man she hardly knew. She raised her eyes. She looked at his eyes, chips of green emeralds. She shivered and gasped for air. Some how, she knew that her fate was with this man, and yet, she knew only fear.

"Yes," smiled Louis, moving his mouth slightly into a short smile, "Yes. I know him quite well. Where is he? He should be with you, his sister. Why is he not here?"

Helen pushed the parasol back and forth. She didn't know if she should be talking to this man that sent the fear chills down her spine. The silence covered her senses. She had to answer. She didn't understand why, but she had to say something. "He, -He jumped off the boat to save some woman he didn't know that was drowning in the water. She had to have fallen from the boat. He gave me his guns and stuff. He should never have jumped into the river. It is dangerous and -"

"Oh," said Louis. "A woman he did not know. So Brave of him. And he left you to fend for yourself? It doesn't sound like McGuire. He is a family men, I thought. Or at least I believed he was."

So something had happened to Clairese. No wonder she wasn't here now. She was caught trying to frame or kill him. So his men did find out about her. Maybe McGuire and Clairese were both dead. What wishful thinking. Nothing so good would happen to McGuire like him to be dead. But he didn't care what happened to Clairese or McGuire right now, he only wanted to know about the angel who stood in front of him. He wanted her. He wanted her badly. Not just her body, but her soul. He was good at getting someone's soul. He wanted her as his queen.

Helen shuffled her feet. "I, I better look to see-"

"No need, we are friends already. We both know your brother, right? I shall take you to where you are going." Louis smile broadened on his face. He felt like laughing. The angel fell right into his lap. He was about to clip her wings so she could not fly away from him. "I even know his address So you see, I really and honestly know Brad McGuire. In fact, you may say we know each other for a very long time. The time of the plantation and white suits. A time that will never come again. A time you might remember as gone. Are you lost? I can ride you to his address."

"No, Oh, No. I can not accept a ride with you. I mean, we both know my brother, but I don't know you. No. I will find a way to go where I have to go." Helen looked at his face quickly. She was afraid if she looked too long, she would turn into stone or maybe salt as the bible preached. Anyways, how could she accept a ride from a Black man? "I- I am not sure of the address. I guess I am really lost."

Louis smiled gently at her. His hand came up, and he gently picked her face up to look at him. He knew he had to go slowly if he was to get what he wanted so badly. She shook as he touched her. He could tell she was about to scream. "Look, I shall let you ride in the carriage to where you are going, and I shall ride outside. That should show you I am no orge. By the way, what is your name?"

Helen tried to close her eyes, but she found herself looking directly into his ice green eyes. She swayed. She swallowed as if she ate something rancid. "I'm Helen McGuire. Brad is my brother. I have just returned from England."

Louis looked into her eyes. Yes, she had a hidden loss there. That was his ace in the hole. He knew he could use that hidden sadness to have her under his control. "I am Louis LaCount. I am at your service. Believe me, if your brother was with you, he would tell you, he knows me very well. Very well indeed. Therefore, I must help you, his sister. Is that not right?"

Helen could not take her eyes away from Louis. She stared at him. She did not know what to do. She could not stand here forever. She had to make up her mind about what to do, but there was no vehicle in sight. She tried to back away from his touch, but he seemed to be glued to her skin. Should she trust this strange man, with the strange eyes that seemed to read her thoughts? There were no cabs in sight. She was so alone without Brad. Yet, she was the old South, and a black man, - to trust him? She stepped further back away from him. She shook her parasol.

Louis smiled for the first time in his life. He knew this was a piece of cake. "Look, I do know your brother. He has hair and eyes the same color as yours, and he is about 6 feet four inches tall, and has broad shoulders, women love him, and he is a gambler. Ask any question about him, and I shall answer it."

Helen tried to smile, yet, something inside of her kept telling her not to get involved with this man. Still, she was tired and wanted to unpack. It was a long trip from England to the Paddle wheeler to here. She was so afraid that Brad was dead. She did not know what she would do if he was dead. She had no place to go. She could not return to England. That way led to Edward, and Edward - well it was over. She had only the money that Brad, her brother won. Was that enough to live on?

She turned and looked all around. She was alone with this black man, and there was no one else to help her. But why would some one help her? She made up her mind she would not stand here forever.

"If you really don't mind, like your riding outside the coach and all." Helen whispered. She glanced at LaCount from her half closed eyes. She had never been alone with a black man. Was he trustworthy? Why would Brad know a black man? It just didn't sit well with her. Brad was old South. But then again, he turned gambler, and maybe a gambler had to know all sorts of men. She was near the end of the wharf and the next step would be into the mud and river. She looked into the ice green eyes of LaCount. She was lost at what to do. There were no cabs. She was not sure of the address Brad had given to her. She was lost and out of her depths. She was never so alone.

Louis smiled, nodded and told his driver to pick up Helen's trunks. They both walked over to his coach. They put the trunks on top of the coach and Louis helped Helen get into the coach. The feel of her hand on his, shook him to the core. His hands were smooth and without callous. His hands were large compared to Helen's hands slim and small. He never felt this way about any woman. Her hand felt like velvet, maybe a plum, soft and ripe. He felt her hand shaking. So, she was afraid of him. That was good, fear was close to love. He would have this woman, and she would be his willing victim.

Louis mounted a black Arabian horse that Helen had not noticed before. He gently patted the horse's head as he turned the horse to be at the window of the coach. He looked in the window and watched Helen. The horse paced himself to keep up with the coach.

Helen sat huddled in the coach. Her dress was bunched around her body, but she did not care. She was so frightened. She kept looking out the window to see if they were still in the city. For some reason, she felt that he would sprint her away. Such a terrible feeling came over her, she could not breathe. Why had she trusted that man? She watched him as he looked into the coach. The horse was beautiful, something like the horses they had on the plantation. How could a black man afford such a horse? Was he a free black man? Was that the new order of things? She had come into a country that she did not know what was up and what was down.

The coach sped across the fields and homes. Some of the homes she noted were on silts Water rising? Or was there another reason? The coach did not stop for any obstruction. It seemed to go on forever like it was possessed. The coach finally stopped and Louise jumped off his horse. He opened the door of the coach. He looked in and saw Helen curled into a ball. Louis stood there with his hand outstretched. She did not want him to touch her hand. He grabbed her hand. She trembled as he took her hand. Helen could feel the hard hand that grasped her little hand. She gulped as she tried to pull away. But the hand lay rock hard around her hand. LaCount pulled her out of the coach. She was a bundle of nerves. Her dress was creased from the ride. She held her head up and tried to act normal, that is as normal as she could be.

She looked around to where they had stopped. They were definitely still in the city. They were in front of a two story house made of wood which came directly to the road. It hardly left room for them to walk up to the house. Louis took her elbow and led her into the road.

Louis felt her shake as he held her elbow and guided her up to the door of the house. He opened the door and they walked up some steps in the hallway.. "See, I am not some type of person that you should show such fear. I feel you shake. Have I hurt you? No.! I help you. I am well known. Everyone knows me. I am very rich and famous. I am sure Mrs. Annabelle Smithy will welcome you. On my say so."

"You really know where Brad lives?" Helene thought back to what Brad had said of where he lived. It sounded like the same place he mentioned. She felt the black man's large hand holding her elbow. She wanted to free her elbow from his grip.

"I'm not sure she knows I am coming. My brother isn't the best of information giver. He likes to keep things to himself." whispered Helen as they reached the door to Mrs. Smithy.

"Do not fear, Mrs. Smithy will take you in gladly," Louis said, as his face once again took on the stern unforgiving look he wore. He knocked on the door. It opened and there was Mrs. Smithy with a surprised look on her face. Mrs. Smithy's heart contracted as she looked at Louis. Did he mean to get rid of her now? But why? She felt her throat tighten with fear. She didn't do anything wrong, did she? Maybe renting to McGuire was the reason for this visit. Why did he bring a woman with him?

Mrs. Smithy did not know what to say. She stood back in complete fear as she saw Louis LaCount at her door. She did noticed the woman next to him. Her mouth formed an "0". Mrs. Smithy pushed her hands into her hair to make it less scrambled looking.

Louis pushed into the house with Helen. "This is Helen McGuire, sister of Brad McGuire, whom you rented a place for room and board. His sister has come to stay with him. I told you about renting a room to McGuire, but you did not listen. Have you any questions?"

Mrs. Smithy wore a old dress of faded blue, and her hair screamed to be combed. She shook in her naked feet. She had not expected a call from LaCount. He had warned her about renting to McGuire, but he left her alone till now. She wanted to vomit. She wanted to scream, I will not rent to McGuire again. I will throw him out if that is what you wish. I do not want trouble. I only rented to McGuire because I needed the money, and you seemed so far away. You knew all the time I rented to McGuire, so why now? What do you want to me?

Helen felt his hand around her waist. She wanted to move away, but the hand was firm. He was like a rock. Her waist burned with his touch. What did he want with all this touching and feeling?

Mrs. Annabelle Smithy just stood there and looked at their backs as they made their way into her house. She didn't dare to say no to LaCount. He owned her house and almost everything that was New Orleans. She rushed in front of the man and woman. She smiled. The girl looked familiar. She had to be McGuire's sister. They had the same colored eyes, lake-blue. The same colored hair-golden. Surely, it was his sister, and what did LaCount want? She had to take a chance. Say she knew it was his sister-then what?

"I am honored to have Brad McQuire's sister stay with us. It is as you wish? I even have an extra room just for her. It was my daughter's room." Mrs. Annabelle Smithy said. Annabelle could feel the fear in her heart begin to quicken. Why would he come here in person, unless it was to evict her? She took a shallow breath.

Louis nodded to Mrs. Smithy, and dropped his hands from Helen's waist. He took Helen's hand into his. "If you need anything at all, just let me know. I am glad Mrs. Smithy has a separate room for you. It is so awkward to be in the same room as one's brother. I would be honored if you would have dinner with me tonight."

Helen looked up at Louis. His ice green eyes beamed into her eyes. Helen looked down at her parasol. "I , I'm too tired tonight. Thanks for asking. But I think I shall go to bed and wonder what happened to Brad and maybe as I am so tired I will fall asleep."

"Yes, that is exactly what I thought you should do. I will pick you up at seven tomorrow night for dinner. In the mean time I shall send out some people to check the river to see if they found your brother. You will like that?" asked Louis

"You will help look for my brother? Oh, my. I was wondering how to get someone to look for him. Please, yes, I do so worry. What ever will I do if he died in the river. He is all I have." Helen said as she looked into the ice green eyes of Louis. "My yes, I shall be honored to have dinner with you. How can I ever thank you?"

Louis bent down and kissed her hand. He straightened up and turned to Mrs. Smithy, "I expect that Miss McGuire will be happy here. I do not intend for her to be some place else. Do you understand?"

Mrs. Smithy "Yes, yes. I'll be sure she is happy. Yes. Is there anything else I can do for you Mr. LaCount?"

Louis turned on his heel and walked out of the room, "By the way, no board for the lady. You understand? I shall see that she has enough to eat. There is no reason for you to give her anything. It that clear Mrs. Smithy? I never repeat myself."

Helen was too tired to notice what he said. She was so tired and so worried. Mrs. Smithy took her arm and led her to a room on the bottom floor Helen noticed they walked in a sort of circle. Leaving the middle of the house out of bounds. She wanted to ask about that, but her brain was whirling around her head. The center of everything was in the circle. They walked in half a circle. Truth?

Mrs. Smithy brought her to a room that was all fluffy and white. It faced out into the street at another house. The bed was covered with a white fluffy bed spread that Mrs. Smithy pulled off and neatly folded it over to the chair by the bed. Helen yawned. A desk was bare with a chair in front of it. A full length mirror stood by the wall. Other than the chair with the bedspread on it, there was nothing else in the small room. Two chairs, a desk a mirror, and a bed.

"This was my daughter's room, when she lived here. She went North. She went with some man and never sent me a word. I do not know if she is alive or dead. I left the room exactly as she left it. This is the room for you to use and whatever-."

"Please excuse me, but I can't keep my eyes open any longer," Helen said as she took off her little high heeled shoes and lay down on the bed.

Annibella Smithy leaned forward and watched Helen as she stumbled into bed with her clothes on. She was sure that Louis was going to want this woman and take her to his home. Mrs. Smithy knew she was a watch dog to see that this woman was here where Louis LaCount came back for her. Annibella Smithy looked down at her bare feet. LaCount knew all the time that Brad McGuire lived here. Was he so sure of everything? He looked like he owned the woman. Was he taking revenge on McGuire? Surely he would take out his hate some where else, besides the woman.

Helen's head whirled as it touched the pillow. She was at a loss to know what to do or say to the black man. He took over so fast her head spun. Maybe if she was not so white he would forget her. Why had he touched her? Why had she let him? Her eyes closed and she fell asleep thinking about what to do and how to do it.

*   *   *

Louis went back to his office. He sat behind a polished oak desk. There was nothing on the top of the desk, but he had drawers stuffed with papers that were very important to his running of New Orleans. He knew every thing he need to know about the people who bowed and scraped to him. He had every secret inside his head. The papers were what he owned. He sat down on his brown leather chair and rang his bell.

His secretary, a man named Joseph Flower answered. He was small, hunched, and his black hair spiked about his round face. His nose dominated his face.

"Sir?" asked Joseph, as he walked silently up to the desk that LaCount sat at.

"Get me the Odge brothers now. Remember, I hate to be kept waiting." said Louis "I also need the big man and the Indian."

Joseph hurried out like an ant ready to attack and sent

a messenger for the Odge brothers to come over quickly. He came back into the office, and bowed slightly. He took a deep breath and said, "They are in the saloon on Main Street, the Three Beggars, I'll find the Indian and the big man shortly. They should be in that fancy apartment you gave them. I don't trust that Big man, but he does what you tell him to do. He has no brains."

LaCount laughed. "That's why I use him. He can't think worth a damn. If I don't have the Indian with him he runs berserk. But the Indian is smart and savvy. He don't stay with the Big man unless I direct him to do so."

Joseph came back shortly and stuck his head into the office. "The Odge brothers are here now. Should I show them in?"

LaCount just laughed, which was strange for him. He held his mirth in. He was getting what he really wanted. The chance to kill McGuire.

In a few minutes the Odge brothers were told to enter the office of LaCount. The were three brothers, all looking like they belonged to some other race than human came into the office. The first brother, Phil was short, squat, had sandy hair, a large nose, and eyes that seemed always closed.

The second brother Amos, was tall, broad, muscular, with a face that looked like a square, with brown hair, brown eyes that popped, and a small mouth.

The third brother, Tom, was fat as a hundred year tree, with a bloated face, ears that stood out like windmills, eyes that remained half closed, with a wide mouth and a nose as red as fire.

Louis looked at the three men standing in front of his desk. These men were born killers. They loved killing anything, dogs, cats, women, children, and men.

"I want you to go up the Mississippi River, with two other men, the Big man and the Indian., and make sure that McGuire and that Clairese are both killed. Can I make myself any clearer. McGuire jumped in the river to save Clairese. They were near Baton Rouge, so that's a start. So where they are now, who knows. But, I want you to make sure that they are never, never found, and they are very dead. Do you understand what I am saying? You three on one side of the river, and the Big man and the Indian on the other side. I want each side of the river covered to be sure they are found and then killed. Get going now and I want no mistakes do you hear me This is important to my plans. .I want them dead, and bring their bodies back to me so I am sure they are dead."

LaCount looked at the men. They hardly looked like killers, but they were known far and wide as the best to slay. He heard them mutter something that sounded almost human and then they turned around and walked to the door.

Louis watched the three men leave his office. He certainly did not want McGuire to be found alive now that he had his sister's life in his lush thoughts. McGuire's sister, the angel who entered his life and made him dream of things he never thought about. Clairese was another matter as far as he was concerned. He was finished with her for good. So he would have to have her killed anyway. This saved time and effort. Without McGuire alive, Helen would have to turn to him. He was the only one she knew, though she feared him. It did not matter, he had found his queen.

He could picture her married to him. Imagine!. Him married. Never thought that would happen, but then he never thought an angel would enter his life. She was perfect for a man in his position to have a wife like her. She was educated, beautiful, and he got a hard on just looking at her. She knew how to run a plantation. She knew how to talk to a president or to a workman. She was flawless as a hostess. She was an impeccable woman to have sex with him forever. She would wear diamonds on special occasions and diamonds when she was without any clothing on just for him. Dreams of her naked with him shook his body. His manhood became rigid. He never thought of children, but with Helen as his wife, he knew he wanted to leave a legacy behind him. He dreamed of having children with Helen, and her knowledge of affairs that mattered. Him most of all!

He was so lucky that Helen just walked into his life and McGuire would be a thing of the past. He hated that man, but his sister, was lovely, desirable, and the one woman that he wanted with all his soul. He never realized that there was something he was lacking, and that was a mate that would be his queen to his king. He had a kingdom for her, and he would give her anything she desired. He found love in the strangest of places. The new mistress he was going to have turned to lie in his thoughts, he could think of nothing else but Helen.

*   *   *

Phil, Amos, and Tom knew the pangs of hunger. They sat in their one room house and waited for their ma to come home. She flitted from man to man and ate where ever the men lived. She never knew the pangs of hunger; she was round and fat. She never laughed at home. She kicked the children. She hated them. They looked as if they came from outer space.

Amos the oldest brother, took care of the other brothers. He never could get his ma to love the kids. He was the only love of his brother's lives. They all had different fathers, so they looked different, but they all had the same ma. Being the oldest, Amos took it upon his self to tell them what to do. Though his eyes popped out, the other two boys knew he was there to help them. They looked up to him as a savor. He was the one who found them food when they were desperate.

They all huddle next to the empty fire place. Thin blankets were wrapped around their shoulders. Amos, tall for his age, shook the brown hair from his face. "The only way we get to eat is to catch it ourselves. Ma will never feed us."

Phil shrugged his shoulders. His sandy hair stood at odd angles to his face. "We don't have a gun."

Amos was seven years old. He lived on scraps where ever he could find them. It was a wonder he lived. It was he who feed the other two boys. Phil was six years old and very short. He was always hungry, yet so little to eat all the time. The little fat brother was Tom. He was five years old and how he became fat was a guess the brother's refused to make. They had an idea but that was all they had.

"Sling shot," said Amos. He liked to see all the dead animals. It was something he could eat. He was too hungry to care what they were. He enjoyed killing because he wanted to exist. It was the only way he had to live.   Kill or die was the only thought he held in his head. Better to kill than to die.

Little fat Tom just sucked his thumb. He never had much to say about anything. But Amos loved him fiercely as he loved his brother Phil. Phil looked at Amos with his eyes half closed. "O.K." was all he said. The brother's never talked much to each other. They understood what had to be done. That was all that mattered in their young lives.

They all looked to see if their Ma had come home drunk as always. She drank anything if it was liquor. She came home, hit the kids and fell onto the floor and lay there among the rags. She never moved until she was ready to go out again and then she would comb her hair and put on lipstick. She never looked at the children. They were just there. That was the extend of her caring for the little children. She often wondered how she got pregnant still she must have been too drunk to think. To think she carried full term, it was a miracle. She made loads of money when she was pregnant. She didn't need to worry about anything than. Knocked up was all she thought and she just went along for the ride.

The boys did not see their Ma as she left the one room shack. She never looked at the boys, and she cared less about them. No beds marred the room, in fact no furniture was in the room. The panes and shutters shone brightly as the door to the shack opened. They had panes and shutters in their room because it came with the room. Otherwise nothing else came with the room, except a deep well of not caring.

"Tom eats rats. That's why he is so fat." said Phil as he walked next to his brother.

"He catches rats? No wonder there are none in our place. Well good for him if he can catch a rat he can have it." said Amos as he laughed and looked at fat Tom Tom just sucked his thumb and looked down at the floor. Then he followed the others out into the sunshine.

"With my sling shot we can get a rabbit or squirrel. Then we can eat. I am so hungry." said Amos as he followed the tracks in the dirt. He was good at tracking, even as a little kid he learned to art of tracking. It was a way of living for him and his brothers.

"Imagine, Tom eating rats raw. That's real hard to think about," said Amos as he tracked the squirrel. "Hard to think about."

The squirrel didn't have a chance with the Odge boys. They were very good at tracking. They caught the squirrel and started a fire. They ate the squirrel and finally sat back and laughed. This was their first time that they felt full in months. The Odge brothers were born to kill in order to live.

It wasn't long after that their mother died. She had a hacking cough. Most nights she kept the boys up, but she never noticed. She was a 'me' generation. She just lay on the rags at home and the boys looked at her. She was dead and they just looked at her and wondered how she would taste.

"Glad she's dead," said Phil. "She hit me for the last time."

"Heck, she was mean, but then so are we. We are the Odge brothers and we stick together no matter what. So our ma is dead, who cares? Let the priest bury her. It's for the best. She never did anything for us." said Amos as he kicked the dead woman in the face. Amos thought of eating her, but then he remembered the priest and he needed to think of the woman who was his mother. Hard to eat one's mother. He let the priest bury her. Still, he thought of how good she would taste. They never talked about eating a person but it was on their minds.

It was seven years later, that Phil came into the shack with a bloody large piece of raw meat and a fat wallet. "Look what I got," screamed Phil

Amos looked at the meat and then the fat wallet. "Where you get the wallet and the meat?"

"I killed this creep and took his ribs for us to eat, and he had a fat wallet from druggies. Why not? We are hungry and a man's meat is as good as a rabbit." Phil proudly said.

Amos took the wallet and counted the money. "Wow, we're rich. I can buy bullets now. We are rolling. We can eat, really eat with this meat from that man."

"We can kill other men who sell drugs. We can kill other men who are alone. We are on top of the world." Screamed Amos.

"Why kill rabbits when we can kill men and eat them. We can track them down when they are alone. We are kings of the world." Phil whispered as he started the fire outside the shack. "We can eat forever."

"Think of the power we can have," said Amos in his normal voice, "We can even make money out of killing. We are rulers of the world. I like that."

Phil smiled and his eyes almost opened. He never wanted to see the world too clearly. He feared the world and what lay in it. He wanted to only eat and do whatever Amos said.

Tom sat on the floor and sucked his thumb. He never wanted for anything except his thumb. His ears flapped in the breeze as he sucked his thumb. His nose, always red, seem to dominate his face. He did not care what they did, he was a follower and follow he did to the best of his ability. Tom wasn't too smart. In fact, he was barely there. He was spaced out from all the rats he ate raw.

It didn't take long, but the Odge brothers got to be famous

for their killings. People were afraid of them. They could wait and trap anyone they wanted. They were good. They started to get money to kill or track someone. They were hired on several occasions to kill or track someone.

They ate real food now. It never tasted as good as the human food they had, but people didn't want to hear about humans being eaten. They gave up eating humans, as the money rolled in. They had a specialty that people wanted. Money was easy to come by. They had a reputation of never failing in what they did. Their reputation grew as the days rolled on. They never became over confident, because Amos made sure that they followed his lead. He knew his brothers were lost without him. Even so, he loved his brothers with a passion. It was strange, because they all had different fathers, but Amos felt compelled to love them, as no one else did. They were ugly, ill used as far as clothing was concerned, and had no manners.

They wore old clothing, that others threw away. They dressed in pants that were torn or worn thin. Their shirts were tattered and had no color. Anyone looking at them would think they were poor, yet they had more money than most of the people who hired them had. The only thing they spent their money on was shelter, a nice apartment with good furniture, and food. They wanted to live in the best of places and they did. Their furniture was made in Europe, and it was classical. The wood rubbed to a rich gleaming brown, and the cushions were soft and felt like clouds. Once in their apartment, one could smell the rich aroma of roses and lilacs. They made sure that their apartment was nothing like the shack they grew up in. The smell was from the petals that were scattered around the room.

Amos knew he deserved the best, and the best was what their apartment held. He would never go back to the shack they had lived in. He made sure that he had plenty of money at all times. He knew his brothers never bothered with money, as they didn't know what to do with it. They were lost without him, and he made sure he took good care of them.

Once in awhile, Phil tried to lead, but Amos shook his head in exasperation. Phil got more out of life with his doing, like killing, then any of the brothers. Phil could not be depended on to think. He was action, and action only. Phil the first to kill someone felt he should be the leader, but Amos took over control of the brothers.

"You can not lead," said Amos as he looked at Phil. "You are a doer, but that is it. Yes, you were the first to kill someone. But it was me, who thought of it as a trade. It was me, who gets the jobs, and its me that says yes or no."

Phil just shook his head. "I am the leader. I am the one who knew to kill a human being. It was me that got the money for a gun. It should be me, that does the thinking and the jobs."

"You want to lead?" asked Amos. "What will you do? Will you ask someone if they want to track someone, or maybe kill them? What do you do to get jobs with money that pays?"

Phil opened his eyes. He was afraid that Amos would kill him. His own brother, but that wasn't possible. Amos loved them. He said so, he thought. "Well, I'm the one who thought of killing, I should be the leader. Everyone should follow me."

Amos took his time in looking at Phil. He sat down on his favorite chair in their apartment. "Was it you that got us this apartment? Was it you that got us these jobs?"

Phil looked down at the floor. There was no reason to argue with his brother. He would never win an argument with Amos.

Tom sat down on the sofa. He was still sucking his thumb. He had less to say than a dummy. He just looked at his brothers and agreed no matter what they said. He had no mind to discuss anything except to do as he was told.

Phil turned around to Tom. "Don't you think I should be the leader? After all, it was me that found a human being to eat. It was me that found the fat wallet? What do you think?

Tom just sat there and finally, he raised his eyes and looked at Phil. He didn't say anything just let his eyes roam over Phil. Tom moved his head and his large ears flapped as he moved. He sat there and said nothing.

Amos was the leader and there was nothing Phil could do about that. Amos was the one who got the jobs, and Amos was the thinker. It was Amos who thought of killing for a living. It was Amos who was the real tracker. It was Amos who had a temper, but kept it hidden from his brothers. It was Amos that worked mostly for LaCount and paid with money that kept the apartment up.

"That's settled," said Amos in a loud voice, "I am the leader. I am the one who people know to come to when they want our services. I am the main person. So Phil, what else do you say?"

Phil looked at the floor as he moved his shoulders in a negative way. "I reckon you are the leader. But I don't see why. I'm just as smart, maybe even smarter. But people do come to you, so I guess you are the leader. I don't want to be a leader anyway."

"I told you why," answered Amos. "I am the brains to this outfit. Get that through your head. I am the leader, and I know what to do. Any questions about that?"

Phil and Tom just stared at the rug. There was nothing more to say to Amos.

"Plus," added Amos, "you all know that I always love you, and I was the one who found the food to make you grow. I am the one who is sure to do right by you. You can trust me, in that."

The two brothers nodded their heads. They trusted Amos with a devotion that was hard to follow. He had kept them alive.

*　　*　　*

32

LaCount looked at his clean desk. It was all he could think about was the coming of the Big Man and the Indian. He remembered the first time he had used the Big Man. It was so embarrassing. The Big Man had no brains. He was a killing machine that did not stop or reason. He had to do something about it, but what?

He thought and thought. The Big Man needed someone who could think. Someone who told him what to do and what not to do. He needed brains. The knock on the door stopped him from thinking of the Big Man because the Big Man was here.

"Come in," said LaCount in his strong voice.

The Big Man came in and stood by the desk. LaCount did not ask him to sit down. LaCount just made his face sterner to look at. His mouth turned into a thin line.

"You disobeyed my orders," said LaCount in a stern voice.

The Big man looked down at his feet. He knew he had done something wrong when LaCount wanted to see him. He did not know what to say or do so he just stared at his shoes.

"Not only do you have no name but you stand like a puppet," scolded LaCount

"I have no name because no one named me," whispered the Big Man.

"Where is the Indian? I told him to look after you." screamed LaCount.

"He hates me," said the Big man.

"You are useless to me and everyone else that needs your services. You killed a dozen people, yet you let the man I wanted dead escape." yelled LaCount

"I just didn't know who you wanted killed," said the Big Man with tears in his eyes. He thought he would go through the floor if LaCount said another word to him. He knew he did wrong. He always did wrong it seemed unless only one person was in the room or by the door for him to kill. He did not know his strength, he only knew he enjoyed putting his hands around a neck and squeezing it until there was no life left in the body.

The Big Man enjoyed seeing the life blood escape from the body. He loved the feeling of power it gave him. Yet, he was afraid of LaCount. He didn't want the ice cold eyes looking at him with disgust. He wanted praise from LaCount not contempt.

"How many times have I told you to do nothing, unless the Indian was with you. You do not listen. I can not trust you to find your feet, you are so stupid." said LaCount as he looked at the Big man.

LaCount glared at the Big Man. There was nothing he could do or say that would change the fact the Big Man did not think. He was useless to use unless he could find a brain for him. It was simple, the brains was the Indian.

LaCount reflected on how he could use the Big Man and still have the use of his brawn. He disliked having tension. He was a man who wanted to have the best of everything, yet he wanted perfection in all parts of his life.

"The only thing I can do for you is give you a brain." said LaCount as his cold eyes looked at the Big Man.

The Big Man shuffled his feet. He didn't dare look up and see how LaCount looked at him.

"I will give you the Indian again." said LaCount in a cool voice. "He is half Indian and half who knows, but he thinks." LaCount continued.

The Big Man wanted to look at LaCount, but didn't dare.

"I have called him to come and see me," LaCount continued. "He will be your brains. You are either with him, or I shall be finished with you. What do you want?"

The Big Man nodded his head. His fear rocked the room. He guessed that if he said no, he would be fish bait. LaCount could move mountains, and the Big man knew he was finished if LaCount said so.

A knock sounded on the door, and LaCount looked at the Big Man. "Answer the door," snarled LaCount. LaCount wondered if the Big man could find the door without a brain to guide him. He watched as the Big man walked to the door.

The Big Man opened the door, and there stood the Indian. The thin, little squirt of a man. His eyes held blood and no remorse. He appraised LaCount and grunted. He would do as he was told. He accepted his fate. He was no stranger to the ways of the world. He stepped into the room and stood very still. Only Indians obeyed the laws of the land. LaCount had told him never to leave the Big man by himself. He was a danger to everyone.

He stood very still and then said, "You wanted to see me?" He knew it had something to do with the Big man. He was in deep trouble.

LaCount looked at the Indian. He hated to use him. He was too talented to be used as the brains of the Big Man, but then, his use was limited. "This Big Man, the one without brains needs a trainer. He is useless to me as he is. He needs someone who can tell him what to do and when. I have picked you as his brains. Do you want the job?"

The Indian squirmed in his moccasins. He understood that if he should refuse, he would end up dead. "Will he listen to me?" asked the Indian How many times had LaCount asked him to baby sit the Big man?

"He'd better," stated LaCount. "I want you with him all the time. At least while we search the land for McGuire and Clarisse. I want them both dead. I want them as dead as can be, never to bother me again. I want their dead bodies brought to me. Do you think you can do that?"

The Indian nodded to LaCount. He could do this. He didn't want to be the Big Mans brains forever, but for a short period of time, he could live through it. Still he knew that LaCount would have him with the Big man forever if he let him.

"Good, its settled. I have the Odge brothers on one side of the river, and you will take the other side of the river. I never want to hear of McGuire or Clairese again." sneered LaCount. "You should be able to kill them without any trouble. I see none. McGuire left his guns with his sister, so he doesn't have any weapons. You have weapons, transportation and the need to kill. Do I make myself clear? Do you need anything further for me to say to you except, kill them. Bring their dead bodies to me, I want to see them dead."

"I have never worked with the Odge brothers before. Are they trustworthy? Can I depend on them? What do they look like?" The Indian shrugged his shoulders and looked directly at LaCount.

LaCount laughed. "One is tall, one is short and the other one is fat. They have worked with me before and they are good. In fact, I would say they are the best that I know of. They don't care who or what to kill, its just a job to them."

"There should be no problem. When do I meet them?" asked the Indian

"Right now," answered LaCount.

He picked up a bell and had it ring. His secretary came in.

"Get the Odge brothers. I want them to meet the Big Man and the Indian. They will be working together. For a short period of time, I hope. One will work one side of the river and the other will work this side of the river. When they find McGuire and Clairese and than they will kill them. I hate to have to tell them what their work is about. I only use them when I want them to kill someone. This time, it is two people that I can't stand the sight of. One slighted me, and the other wanted me dead."

The Odge brother came in and stood at attention. They listened to what LaCount had to say and they nodded their heads in agreement. The Big Man and the Indian watched their reaction.

36

The Indian watched the Odge brothers. They looked so strange and different, from the human race. They told him they had different fathers, they still looked strange. They had a reputation of being capable of killing when told who and where. He could depend of that. He hated being teamed with the Big Man. The Big Man had no brains to speak of and the Indian was all brain and no brawn. So many times LaCount had asked him to watch over the Big man. It was like watching paint dry. He had no choice but to accept this assignment. LaCount would make him, the Indian, disappear in a second.

The Indian though about his parents. His father was brilliant, and yet, he was kicked out of his tribe because he was a freak. He was too little, he was to skinny and his head was way to big for a human. The Indian could not prove he was born into the tribe, because his parents, as they were dead. They had died out on the plain and he was left with his grand mother. She brought him up, but even she was ashamed of him. He was so odd. She hid him most of his growing up years.

At the tender age of eighteen he left the tribe that never wanted him, as they looked at him as a freak. He roamed around until he hit New Orleans, and then he stayed. For no reason, except it seemed not to notice him. He looked around and found he could use his brains to make people disappear when he wanted them to. He finally found a job with LaCount and stayed with him, even though LaCount could not look at him with respect. He was human and he wanted sex, but no woman would look at him. He was a freak, small, skinny, and with a big head, that housed his brains.

The Indian saw her sitting on her porch with a frown on her brow. She looked like a mountain of lumps and bumps. He knew she did not know what sex was. Who would have her? He had found the woman who would serve his needs. He needed sex and the feel of wonder. He wanted a baby to teach him or her the beauty of the brain. He wanted so much to be normal.

They were so different from each other, the Indian and the Mountain woman. It was a wonder that he was conceived. He thought of his mother. She was a big woman, tall and round and really big. She could have been in the circus, she was so huge. She seldom smiled, because she had nothing to smile about. She usually had a big frown on her face. No one liked her, and she hated everyone she met or saw. She was a loner, a person who wanted and needed to be alone.

His father was a small man. He was built like a stick. More like he was, small and brilliant. How he ever met his mother, he was not sure, but meet they did. His father, the Indian, his mother a white woman like a boulder. His father looked at the white woman and decided that she was what he wanted and needed.

They met in New Orleans, the city of dreams. His father wanted this huge white woman, and she, a brainless twit, did not know what to think. No one wanted her. She was sure of that, but the Indian wanted her. Where he came from and where he would go she did not know. She only knew he wanted her and he wanted her as his own as long as he was in town.

He courted her as if she was human. He gave her feathers and he gave her stones. He gave her his warm smile. She never had anyone smile at her before. She was in awe of him. She knew she could make ten of him, but he was there and always smiling. She closed her eyes, and she believed that someone would want her. She knew she was a monster but he loved her, she was sure of that.

"You are here again," she said as she looked at him. "Is there any reason you are here?"

"I am here because of you. You know that," said the Indian.

"I know nothing. I am a huge woman and no one wants me," she replied.

"Ah, I want you. You are what I am looking for. You are

more woman that any of the woman I have see. You are just what I need." the Indian said.

"What you need," said the white huge women. "What am I some special project that you are working on?"

"No," said the Indian. "I need someone who will appreciate me. I need someone who will give me a child. I need someone that will be mine, and mine alone."

For the first time in her live, the big white woman smiled. She could not believe what she heard. She hardly breathed. She stared at the thin Indian. Could it really be that someone wanted her, her alone?

"We can go to bed now," said the Indian.

"You want me," whispered the woman.

"No one else will do," replied the Indian.

"You have a reason for this love?" asked the woman.

"Yes," said the Indian. "I need to love someone and you are it."

"If I lay on top of you, there will be no more you," smiled the big white woman.

"I shall go on top of you, then we will be fine," said the Indian.

"Have you a name?" asked the big woman.

"No, I am a freak," said the Indian in despair.

"I am a freak also," said the big woman with tears in her eyes.

They went to bed and for days they were together, except when the Indian had to work for LaCount. He would excuse himself and then he would disappear. He would come back to be with the big white woman who looked like a mountain.

She had the baby, and the Indian looked at it. "It looks like Me." he cried as the tears leaked out of his eyes. "He will never have a chance to live right. He is almost a stick and here he is a new born baby."

"Maybe he'll change," said the big woman. "It's only a baby."

"No," said the Indian. "He will be an outcast just like me."

It was months later, to be exact, it was nine months, when the Indian took the baby to raise him himself. It would not let the fat white woman near his child. He would teach the child himself and he would name him Wind of the Wild. He would not let another child into this world without a name as he was without a name. Only name he was called was the Indian. It was not right, but there was nothing he could do about it. He taught his son how to use his brain. He taught him how to go unnoticed. He taught him all that he could until the child was nine years old. Then he told him he had lived enough, and the child had to know what to do. They went to Lake Ponsetrain, and there the old Indian slit his wrists and let the blood run into the lake.

"I am old and of no use to anyone," said the Indian

"What am I to do?" asked the child.

"You will get older and then you will work for LaCount. He is a tough one to work for and he does not uses anyone that make mistakes."

"But father, how will I live for now?" asked Wind of the Wild.

"You will find a way. I have taught you all that you need to know. Now it is time for you to look after yourself. Do not go to your mother, she is a nothing, a lump of coal. You must survive on your own," said the Indian as he slowly died.

Wind of the Wild ate from garbage cans and did chores until he was eighteen, then he went to work for LaCount. He was better than the best men that LaCount had working for him. The Indian was perfection. Everyone wanted Wind of the Wild, but he would not tell them his name. He went by the Indian as his father had gone by, and so people called him The Indian.

He never went near his mother, but he heard she had died after the Indian left her. She had nothing to live for after he left. She finally knew what sex was like, and she adored it.

The Indian's reputation became a legend while he lived. Therefore, he was not too eager to work with the Big Man, without brains, and the Odge brothers who were not what he would depend on. He liked to work alone and then he knew what he would do, with all these new bodies, he was not sure of what would happen. He nodded his acceptance to what he could not change, and went to the brothers.

He knew in his heart and soul that something bad would happen to him with all these raw men. They were not thinking men he could tell. He had no choice, except to obey the orders of LaCount. He walked over to the brothers and the Big Man.

"We work together," the Indian said, and still did not tell his name.

"Together," said Amos "but just for this one job." Amos did not trust working with someone he did not know. He only had faith in his brothers.

The Big Man just smiled. The Indian did not know what to do with all these people. He was use to working alone, or with only the Big man when directed to do so by LaCount.

The five men left LaCount together. They had gear to get and weapons to sharpen and sort. They didn't look at each other, but they knew they had a job to do, and do it they would. They also had to plan how to keep in touch with each other on their side of the wide Mississippi. It was important on which side the group would go.

Chapter III

McGuire smashed into the water in a perfect dive. The cold of the water seeped through his clothing and into his bones. He looked around to see where the woman was who had fallen, or been pushed into the water. The paddle wheeler was chugging along in front of him now. He saw the woman from the corner of his eye. She was gong down.

McGuire swam with the current over to where she was last seen and dived into the murky water. He felt the water rage against his body. Trees came bubbling down the river missing him by inches. McGuire saw her hair streaming up in the water. Nothing else was visible, just her hair. Forcing himself his cold aching body to move, McGuire swam with all his might to where he saw her hair. McGuire pulled her brown hair and she came trailing up. Her skirts kept pulling her down into the water. The skirts balled out like wet balloons. She wore a wide skirted dress with maybe three petticoats. The dress was a dark crimson and remaindered McGuire of LouLou who was his mistress back in Cactus Gulch. The neckline of the dress was cut very low, so her breasts could be seen. Her eyes were closed and she seemed to have lost the ability to live. She didn't seem to be alive.

McGuire took the knife he always carried around his

waist. He opened it and then dived into the water, but he still held her hair with one hand. He made sure her face stayed out of the water. He cut her skirt in half, turned her around and cut the other half. He then took his knife and cut the bodice of her dress in half, and turned her, still holding her head above water by her hair, cut the back of her blouse and peeled off her clothing. Carrying her with him. he dived in and pulled her petticoats off. This was an almost impossible task, but McGuire accomplished getting her petticoats off before they dragged her down again.

The woman spilled water from her large mouth. Her black-gray eyes closed and opened. Her eyes were fringed with very long, black lashes. She closed her eyes again. McGuire pulled her under his arms and started to swim in the swift current. He angled towards shore, but big trees floating all around him almost caused him to loose his hold on the woman when he almost crashed into one.

Instead of worrying about the trees hitting him, he grabbed hold of a tree with one arm. He pulled the woman closer to his body as protection from other debris floating down the river. She was dead weight in his arm. She was so lax that McGuire worried if she lived.

The tree bumped along the river and McGuire was starting to tire, as he held the tree and the woman. As luck would have it, the tree hit another large tree, which angled his tree into the side of the slow going river. Once close enough to the river side, McGuire quickly let go of the tree and swam with the woman towards shore. He hardly believed he had made it in the raging river. Lady Luck must have been with him to let him live.

He waded to shore, dragging the woman by her waist. He was so tired, he just lay down in the mud to catch his breath. He made sure the woman lay with her face up. He breathed deeply of the air. The woman stirred in the mud. The woman gagged and then spit out more water from her mouth. She was like a fountain, water spilled out of her mouth.

He almost laughed looking at the woman. She had on only a pair of pantaloons and a chemise. Her hair looked like it was sea weed as it spread around her face. She wasn't bad looking. Not something he would want, but nice looking even after her almost drowning. McGuire sat up and stared around him.

McGuire put his hands in back of his head and just breathed with his eyes wide open. He ran his hands through his hair. Where was he? What to do were questions he would ask himself later. Here he was with only stockings on, no guns, only a knife, no shoes, and some strange woman who was thrown overboard. Or maybe, hopefully fell in. What a mess for a man like him. But, he always had to be around to save some fair lady. Never again would he fall for a fair lady. That was his undoing What was wrong with him? Didn't he learn his lesson with Samantha?

His golden hair fell over his face when he looked up at the sky. Slowly he turned his head.. He looked at the woman and noticed she was staring at him.

"We're in a mess," McGuire said. "I don't know where we are, except we passed Baton Rouge. I don't know how to get to New Orleans. I'm not a river man. Guess we follow the river flow it goes to New Orleans. I have no shoes, you have shoes or boots on. In fact, you have no dress. I don't even know who you are and why they threw you into the river. Maybe hopefully you just fell in? Right now, I am hungry and I don't know where we will get anything to eat. I am also very cold, and I do not know how to build a fire. Have you any questions?"

"What happened to my dress and petticoats, " asked the ragged lady. "Plus I am hungry also, and very cold. You saved my life."

"Well, sister, it was a question of saving you, or saving your dress and petticoats. I figured you wanted to live, so I cut your dress off with my knife, and pulled your petticoats off," McGuire answered.

The woman sat up. The mud covered her arms and the

back of her whole body. "I am full of mud. I think I'll go wash it off in the river."

"Fine, Just remember I only rescue people once. The rest is up to you. I am too tired to worry about mud right now. In fact, I'm going to lie here for awhile until I feel up to moving," said McGuire.

McGuire started to think. What had he done? He left his sister to the mercy of luck. The lady he rescued didn't look like she wanted help or maybe she wanted to die.

His mind whirled around as he thought of his sister. She was always a ray of sunshine. Now, she moped around as if it was hard to live. What had gone wrong in England? It had to be the time she left and the time she came to him. What had gone wrong, he asked himself again? He could not think of what he had done. He had jumped into the water to save the lady. But really he wanted to be rid of his sister. He did not want the responsibility of having her live with him. He thought of dieing. He thought of responsibility. He thought of the time they had together as children. He understood he left her, so he would not be responsible for her. He suddenly wanted to die because he left her so alone. He did not think for the moment in time that it took to jump into the water. What a fool he was!

He looked at the woman. She looked good even half dressed. She carried herself with pride. He noticed her shoes or where they boots? She moved slowly as the mud sucked at her boots. They were high button boots with a high heel. Not a normal outfit for a lady. Or was she a lady? He noticed her try to lift her foot from the mud,. But it sucked her as a living thing.

She shook her head in wonder of her shoes or boots. She did not move now at all. She tried to lift her foot and the mud made it impossible. She was like a wax figure stuck in glue paper.

"Take your boots off," cried McGuire in a loud voice.

She looked at him in wonder. "What do you mean? I can not go without my boots on. It is unseemly."

"Do you like being stuck in the mud?" asked McGuire.

She sat down in the mud and removed her boots. She look like she was going to cry. "I can't walk barefoot. I never have since I was little girl."

"It's that or stay left behind. I'm not waiting for you. In fact, I don't know what reason I had for saving you. I must be nuts." stated McGuire as he shoved his hands into his trousers and sat up straight. He stood up and looked around the land. Every where there was mud, and tree far inland, and maybe animals that were hungry.

She looked at him and knew he meant to leave her behind. "Don't leave me, please, I don't know how to survive in this wilderness."

"Truthfully nether do I," stated McGuire. "Not in land like this. I never seen anything like it."

"I'm a city girl," said the woman. "I never left the city. What can we do?"

McGuire just stared to her. She seemed suddenly quite pretty. Was it the sun setting in the West? Or had he just left his mind on the paddle wheeler?

The woman went to the river, and put one foot in and then the other. She quickly put the rest of her body in near the edge of the river. Not getting too much mud off of her, she just shrugged and came back to where McGuire stood.

"What are we going to do?" asked the woman.

"I don't know yet, but I guess I'll get up and think of something. We know New Orleans is South, and the river is flowing to New Orleans., so we follow the river. That is the best thing I can think of. Let me rinse myself off in the river and we start to walk." McGuire said. "I must have my head examined. Why did I save you?"

"It was fate. It was meant to be," said the woman.

McGuire walked to the river and rinsed himself off at

the edge. He pushed back his golden hair and looked around. There was nothing to see but trees, mud and water. Evening was setting in, and McGuire knew there were water moccasins around, and he sure had no shoes nor did the woman have shoes. They had to be careful where they walked, or they might not make it at all. Snakes were funny, but hopefully they slept at night.

The river raged and foamed like an angry beast. There were trees floating down the river, and Brad could see the top soil that mixed with the water. It looked like a stew to him. He also noticed the things he could not name that seemed to be part of the water. The sun made the water shine as red gleams and silver mixed with the blue and black of the water. It was not lost on Brad that it seemed a hopeless task to compete with the river. He shook his head in wonder that he had jumped into this mess with both eyes opened. He did it because he could not look at his sister again. There was something so tragic about looking at her.

McGuire walked back to the woman. "I think we find a tree to sleep in for the night. Glory be, who knows what is out here. Hear bears are around here, for sure snakes, so lets find a tree to sleep in and then in the morning start to walk to New Orleans. Have you a better idea?"

The woman shook her head. "I'm cold." Then she blinked her black-gray eyes and her lashes swept over her cheeks. Her large breasts strained against her chemise. She knew she was a beauty without anyone telling her. She looked at him and hoped he noticed how good-looking she was. She was use to men trying to win her just to hear her laugh. She never was untrue to LaCount, and yet, she knew he was trying to get rid of her. He was tired of her. She really and truly loved that man. She looked at McGuire and saw his golden hair. She smiled to herself, another conquest.

McGuire was not looking at her. He stared at the barren trees and mud. He certainly was a fool and he knew it. Being left with a woman who was known as a lf as a beauty and there was nothing to keep warm or anything to eat.

"Got news for you sister, I'm freezing. But there is nothing I can think of that we can do. Best sleep in a tree, dry up, and we got a lot of walking in this mud by the bank. If we leave the bank, we might get lost. Then we can wonder around till we die. I think I can face my sister again. I left her alone on the boat. I wonder what she will do. I am a coward."

Both of them pounded through the mud looking for a tree they could sleep in. Finally, they found a tree with branches that were thick, close together, and near enough to the ground so they could reach it. They climbed the tree not talking to each other.

The woman was disgusted that McGuire did not give her a tumble. At least a smile, she thought. She was use to being wanted.

McGuire pushed his back against the trunk of the tree and twined his legs around the branch. He took a deep breath and closed his eyes. The woman followed suit. It took awhile for them to fall asleep as they both felt the cold churning their bones. Though they were cold, they were exhausted and needed their rest. Finally thinking of bears and snakes, and maybe other wild animals they dozed off. The night wore on and nothing untold happened. They did not fall off the tree, nor did any wild animal come to taunt them.

The sun came up through the trees. It was high in the sky when McGuire woke up. The woman was still asleep, leaning against the trunk of the tree in a crook of where two branches came together. McGuire jumped off the tree and then reached up and shook the woman.

"Time to move," McGuire said. "We can't sleep forever."

The woman looked around and almost fell out of the tree. She looked at McGuire and slowly gathered herself enough to jump off the tree.

"I am so cold and hungry. What are we to do?" asked the woman.

"Can't think of anything right off. We do have a knife and we have no shoes, so watch where you step. There are snakes around." said McGuire as he looked at the Mississippi River rolling along. "Snakes like to sun themselves by the river."

"I'm hungry," said the woman "I'm so cold. I'm so hungry. I want to die."

"Tell me something I don't know. What do you think I am? Let's walk as much as we can in this mud and then think of something we can do to eat and drink."

"Can't we drink from the river?"

"Can't think of anything else to do. Have to use our hands. Be sure not to put your face in the river. That current is tough and can drag you back into the water."

"I miss my boots," said the woman as she looked at her bare feet. "I haven't gone barefoot for so long."

"You're Lucky to be alive, so stop the belly aching. If I hadn't saved you, you would be fish bait by now." replied McGuire.

The walked towards the edge of the river in slow motion. It was hard walking in the mud. Every time they lifted their foot, mud would slid down their legs. They just trudged along.

They both reached the edge of the river bank and using their hands, drank the water from the river. Slopping into the mud, they started to walk. It was hard work walking in the mud. They did not talk. The woman started to walk ahead of McGuire as McGuire was looking over the land.

`'"Wait," cried McGuire. He saw the woman almost stepped on a water moccasin. Taking his knife out he aimed it and threw it at the snake. The knife sliced into the snakes head. The snake wreathed and then was still. The woman bent double and started to cry.

"It's no use," she cried. "We will never reach New Orleans. We don't even know how far away it is. We can't step into this mud. There are snakes, and who knows what else. We might as well use your knife to kill ourselves."

McGuire came over to the snake. He kicked it with his feet. The snake did not move. "Well, we got something to eat any way. Wish we could build a fire. Tastes better if the snake is cooked."

The woman looked at him. "Eat the snake?"

"You got a better idea?" asked McGuire as he pulled his knife out of the head of the snake. Cut the head off, and then started to skin the snake. "Ate snake in Arizona. Tastes like chicken, at least rattlers tasted that way."

The woman watch fascinated. McGuire cut the snake into small pieces. "Here, have a piece."

"I can't eat that." cried the woman. "I would rather die than eat a snake. Especially a raw snake."

"You will eat it, when you get hungry enough." McGuire bit into the snake meat. He chewed and chewed and finally swallowed. "Not bad. Takes away the hunger mighty quickly." Then McGuire thought. "Lets get some of those dry little branches over here. I think the sun on my knife might make a fire."

They gathered small branches that were dry. McGuire shone his knife on the branches. Nothing happened. He kept shinning the sun off his knife. A puff of small smoke started in the dry branches. McGuire fanned the branches. The fire took over the brittle branches. McGuire put the snake meat on a stick and held it over the fire. The snake meat sizzled. McGuire cooked all the meat on sticks.

'Here, no try this," McGuire said as he held out a stick to the woman.

The woman took the snake meat on the stick. She put it near her mouth and stared at the snake meat. She shrugged her shoulders and put a piece of the meat in her mouth . Her stomach started to rumble but she chewed the meat. Finally she swallowed the snake meat. Her nose wrinkled as the meat went down.

"It does not taste like chicken," said the woman with a lofty air.

"We'll save the rest of the meat for when we are very hungry." McGuire said as he took some leaves and wrapped it round the snake meat. He ignored the woman as much as he could under the circumstances.

"You are right. When we are very hungry. Boy, that meat makes me want to puke. But like you say, save it for when we are hungry." Clairese said "Actually, maybe it tastes a bit like chicken."

They walked in silence. Dragging their feet through the mud. "I can't go any further without a rest," the woman said in a soft voice.

McGuire stopped and they moved away from the mud and into the trees. They Still kept sight of the river. They both sat down on the grass.

"Want some more snake?" asked McGuire

"Please," said the woman. She took the wrapped snake in the leaves. She pealed the leaves back. She started to eat the snake meat. "You haven't even asked my name. You saved my life, aren't you the bit interested in my name at least?"

McGuire shook his head. "Yeah, I sure would like to know your name, and why they threw you into the river. I really don't want to know too much about you. I had that experience before and I don't want a repeat of saving a woman and then falling in love with her to be rejected because she found someone better."

McGuire looked at the woman sitting next to him and took in every inch of her.. Her hair was very curly and stone brown. He noticed her eyes were large and wide apart and the color of black-gray clouds. Surprisingly, the lashes to her eyes were a deep black and very long, making her eyes stand out. She had a large mouth for her small face. Her coloring was golden like honey. Put all together, she was attractive, even though she was ragged from the river and the wilderness. He noticed she had large breasts and a tiny waist. She was about five feet two inches tall.

"My mane is Clairese. That's it. No other name. Never had a second name. Seems kind of crazy, but true. If you are wondering what I am, I am half white, and half black. So have you something to say to that?"

McGuire looked at her and laughed. "What do you want me to say?"

Clairese huffed. McGuire waited for the rest. "Well, go on girl, Why did they throw you into the river?"

Clairese stood up. "Not now, maybe later I'll tell you. I guess you deserve to know, but not now. I have to think about what happened and I don't know you at all."

McGuire stared at her with his lake-blue eyes. "Hell lady, I don't know you at all either, and I told you, I don't want to know you."

McGuire stood up and they angled back to the river. This time they tried to walk near the trees, but there was too much underbrush to be successful. They finally went back to the mud around the river and started to walk. They walked without talking until the sun started to sink in the West. Once again they looked for trees nearby that could support them over night.

Before the light was completely gone, they found a large tree with wide branches, but better yet, they saw a turtle. McGuire quickly grabbed the turtle by its shell and stuck his knife into the soft meat. A head popped out of the shell with mouth wide open. McGuire made sure he didn't put his hands near that head. Probably a turtle that would eat him alive. He sliced the head off.

"Wow, we now have turtle to eat." McGuire gave a happy laugh. "Maybe we're near something we can tell how far we've gone. Well, I'd say, Lady Luck is with us. We don't starve, and we have a handy tree."

Clairese looked at McGuire. "We'd be a lot warmer if we slept together. Why do you keep yourself so far away from me. I'm not that bad looking."

"You know you're beautiful. But I don't want temptation. I want to be by myself. No regrets, no wonders, and no woman." McGuire said in a shaky voice.

"You regret it right now," said the strange woman. "I can tell when a man wants a woman."

"Maybe, but I'll live a long life without complications." said McGuire.

McGuire looked at Clairese. She was a pretty thing, but, he swore he would have nothing more to do with woman. He was no play thing. Seems all the woman he had made love to wanted his penis, but that was all. It was theirs to play with and admire. They loved his body and his looks. Well, those days were gone. The one woman he wanted didn't want him. No sir, even after he had her in the bed. She enjoyed the fun and games, but when it came down to the wire, like marriage, well, she just took another.

"Is it because I am black and your Southern?" asked Clairese

"Hell, no," replied McGuire

He shook his head at Clairese. "I'm in no mood to get entangled with a woman. Lest of all you. Why the hell did they throw you in the river. They sure wanted you dead. They knew there was no way for you to save yourself."

Clairese looked down at the ground. Her huge eyes looked up into McQuire's lake-blue eyes. "I'm just cold. Can't we at least sleep next to each other?"

"No!" said McGuire as he pulled the shell off the turtle. He cast the shell down into the mud. "No, I'm not getting involved in anything any more." He squashed the pale skin he held in his hand. Then he thought better of it, and smoothed the body of the turtle out.

Clairese smiled. Her large mouth opened and she laughed, and laughed. "You poor fool, you are involved more than you know. You want to know why they threw me in the river? Well, my fine, well, meaning friend, that is why you are involved. You saved this poor person's ass."

53

"So- Seems to me you should be glad I saved your ass. If you want to speak in that base language." McGuire snarled as he squatted down on the ground and wrapped the flesh of the turtle in some grass.

Clairese shook her chemise. Her large breasts filled the flimsy cotton. Clairese looked at the turtle flesh. She felt her stomach turn in revolt. She hated all this rot stuff she had to eat to live. She hated the mud the clung to her skin like a second snakes skin. She hated the idea that McGuire didn't find her attractive and want her.

"They wanted to kill me," Clairese said.

"I would never guess," shouted McGuire "Not often someone is throw into the river. It's a shame I was there. Seems my luck to be in the wrong place at the right time."

"Listen, loosen up and be quiet. I bet Louis sent some one out here to kill me. They'll kill you because you are just here."

"You mean Louis LaCount has something to do with all this?" asked McGuire

"You can bet your sweet life he does," answered Clairese.

McGuire stared into the river. He watched the pattern of the last of the sun ripple in the water. He could smell the stench of mud in his nostrils. Was it because of LaCount he was here in the wilderness. He felt helpless as he didn't know what he had fallen into. His passion of hate stirred his soul. LaCount, the man was cruel, and mean, and most important of all, he was crooked. There was not a straight bone in his whole body.

He hated that man with a passion. He had almost fought a duel with him about his accusations. He had dared to claim he saw him cheat. McGuire cheat. Never. He played with Lady Luck his only woman friend and lover. He would never cheat. He challenged LaCount to a duel. LaCount was smart and smooth, and he got out of saying anything was wrong. He certainly was misunderstood, he said, he never meant McGuire cheated.

No, no, he never said McGuire cheated. No, it was the other player he was talking about. But he saw the cold ice green eyes of LaCount. LaCount was going to kill him, McGuire. He hated him because he made him back down. Sure, he saw the silver guns he carried. He never hid them. He loved his silver guns. LaCount knew he could shoot, and shoot to kill. Everyone knew he could shoot and kill at a moments notice. It was the way he challenged LaCount.

Yes, it was the way he challenged LaCount with the knowledge that he was going to kill him. McGuire could see LaCount knew about his aim with guns. He heard about his temper. He knew they were now sworn enemies and that would never change. McGuire hated him because he called him a cheat and didn't accept the challenge. LaCount hated him because he had the nerve to challenge him.

He looked at Clairese. She stood leaning against the tree they were going to sleep in that night. Clairese smiled and her large mouth wanted to laugh. He could see how hard it was for her to keep from laughing.

"O.K., so you know LaCount wants to kill you. But do you know, he wants to kill me also. Remember the game of cards at one of the saloons in New Orleans. You heard talk abut it, I'm sure. Well, remember he said some one was a cheat. That was me. No one calls me a cheat. I challenged him to a duel. He looked at my silver guns and backed out of it. Coward! He only wins in the underhanded way he lives."

"He backed out?" asked Clairese. "He never backs out. He also always get even with who ever he hates. He's not nice in any way. He hates with a passion. I don't think he loves anyone but himself."

"Sure as we're in trouble and up to our butts in mud," laughed McGuire. "He hates my guts. He hates everything about me. I won't be surprised if he has men gunning for us. What a pleasure it will be for him to find us dead."

Clairese moved over to where McGuire now stood. She put

her arms around his neck. "Come on, let's live a little. We may be in our graves tomorrow. I'm sure LaCount sent someone to find us and kill us if the river did not get us and we are still alive. Not even that, I think he sent men on each side of the river to be sure we are dead. Really dead, by the river or by him."

"No one knows I jumped in to save you, but my sister Helen." said McGuire

"Maybe she inadvertently told someone. Maybe her land lady. Maybe a taxi driver. Maybe she didn't know what to do and told a copper." Said Clairese. "He knows you jumped in after me. But you can bet your life, LaCount knows we are together and alive."

"You think?" McGuire looked at the river and stared at the water as it flowed past him

"I'm sure. There are loads of people on the boat. Someone must have seen you jump. Someone saw them throw me over and into the water." Clairese put her large mouth next to McGuire. She licked his lips. She put her mouth next to his and kissed him. She hugged him tighter. "I'm so scared."

McGuire put his arms around her waist. He felt how small her waist was. He could circle it with one hand. He felt her breasts against his chest. She rubbed her breasts against his chest. Her fingers opened his shirt. She felt his bare chest. Her fingers played with his hair on his chest. Her eyes glittered as she looked up into his lake-blue eyes.

He bent down and kissed her hard. He felt the desire in her body quiver. She closed her black-gray eyes. She entwined her body around his like ivy. Her bare foot trailed down his foot.

McGuire shivered. He loved the ladies. Oh, how he loved the ladies. But his misadventure with Samantha had cooled his longing to be with a woman. He could feel his body burn as Clairesse seemed to melt into his body. Clairese put both her hands on his hair. She gently pulled his hair until his face looked at hers. His deep lake blue eyes delved into her eyes. They stared at each other.

Clairese never saw any man as beautiful as McGuire. If only his eyes showed a bit of like for her she would not feel so depressed. She could see the burning desire she had created in his body. But his eyes, looked so, sad, and lonely.

Clairese laughed into his face. "If only I could have been there and seen all this great stuff happen between you and LaCount. I bet that is something he will never forget. I know you can care less, but LaCount as an enemy! He is like sticking your head into a barrel of rattle snakes."

McGuire laughed. For the first time he felt free and easy. He didn't care how long it took them to get to New Orleans. He hugged Clairese with tender might. He bent to kiss her large mouth. Then a stab of guilt. His sister, Helen, oh, my, he had to get there quickly to New Orleans. He was responsible for her. What had he been thinking?

He certainly could not think he could play around and make time. Helen would be on her own with no one to help her.

What had Helen done when she found herself alone? How safe was she? Would LaCount find her and do something revolting to get even with him? He kept thinking about what he told her where he lived. He could not picture Helen remembering what he had told her. He could see her wondering all over New Orleans and not knowing what to do or where to go.

He looked again at Clairese. It was near night and he was just too tired to go on walking. There was nothing he could do right now to help his sister. But he felt his manhood becoming hard. He wanted to feel Clairese' flesh around him. He wanted to suck her large breasts.

Clairese looked at him with her dark eyes. They gleamed in the light of the night. She let McGuire go, but she stood near him, so he could smell her flesh and want.

She moved up to him and put her arms around his neck. He pulled her closer as her breasts rubbed against his chest. He pulled his shirt off and pulled her chemise down. She rubbed her breasts slowly at first and then she rubbed her whole body against his. He pulled her down into the mud and sucked her breast. Then he kissed her large mouth. His hands went wild about her body. He knew to need of his body and wanted satisfaction now. His hand went into her platoons. He felt for her secret place of love.

His tongue played with hers as they kissed. His hand gently rubbed her woman's love place. She opened up his pants a button at a time. She stroked his penis with her long fingers. He could feel the fire in his body. He pulled her closer to his body. Her hair tickled his nose. He brushed her hair from her face and quickly kissed her again.

Her skin felt like soft down, inviting him to come into her. He gently swung her over on her back. He looked deep into her eyes. She smiled up at him with an inviting sigh. He pulled her platoons off. He pulled her hand away and he plunged into her depths. He was wrapped in the warmth of her heavenly body. They strained and rolled in the mud. He could feel the mud come between their bodies, but it was like a sexy bath. He cupped her face in his hand and kissed her again. He felt his body stiffen with pleasure and Clairese quivered at the same time.

They looked at each other as he still lay in her. McGuire finally pulled away from her. He was not alone, he was a man who found a partner and was filled with the desire he felt for her. Too long had he been alone. Samantha was past, and he had to live life in the present. He had to take charge and be ready to fight and love. Too long had he refused to listen to his brain and find a new love. Not that Clairese would be his new love, but it was close. He had to remember he loved all the ladies equally.

He remembered his life on the plantation and all the things he took for as his God given right. First there was always money to burn. He never worried about money. Now, all he ever did was worry about money

Second he was secure in his way of life. He never dreamed it would end in disaster. How could his life be just ended when he was ready to begin it? The war was horrible. He hated every moment of the war, but he learned how to survive. He came to realize that life was to be played like a game. Men died and were maimed. Prisons held no promise of life. They were without doctors or nurses and most important- food. A time to forget and never think back. The past was over and done with, and it was time he lived his life now. But he was a hunted man according to Clairese. LaCount would kill him if he could. He must use all his mental abilities to help Helen and live. The time had come for him to be ready for anything under the sun where LaCount was concerned.

Chapter IV

BRAD MCGUIRE WENT INTO THE fanciest Saloon in New Orleans. His pockets jingled with gold coins. He felt the sweet kiss of Lady Luck on his brow. He knew when he felt this kiss his luck would be fantastic. In fact, he felt like Lady Luck was more of a real person then the people who walked the streets. Brad McGuire was dressed all in white. He was young and he was handsome. Every woman in the world would do anything he wanted. He knew it. He smiled wide and big. He had the whole world in his power.

He was heir to the large plantation in Carolina, He was rich; he was handsome; he thought the world turned on him. His Father had sent him to New Orleans to get his full of women and gambling. Time to settle down was his father's refrain. Well, maybe it was time, but he hadn't found a woman he wanted to wed and have babies with. Still, why worry about that now. He was here for fun. He was here for wine, woman and gambling.

He looked over the gaming tables in The Bell Saloon. He found one that needed another player. He went over. He was about to sit down, when he noticed one of the players was colored. Brad did a quick back track and walked away. Man, he wasn't about to play with a black man.

He knew he was in deep trouble when he glanced at the

black man. But hell, he was a Southerner and one did not sit and play with a black man. How did he know if he was a run away slave or a free man? Not that Brad cared, he was on holiday, and that was all he thought about.

The black man shoved his cards away and stood up, his green eyes gleamed like a wolves. Swift as a cougar, the man laid his hand on McGuire's white coat. McGuire shook his hand off his coat as he turned to face the man.

"What's the matter? You don't think I'm as good as you?" The black man's cold green eyes took Brad's measure.

Brad laughed. His white teeth gleamed in the dull light. "Nothing is the matter. I just don't play with black men. Personally, I don't know if your a good poker player or not. It's just what I do. Don't want to play with you. For all I know, you're a run away slave."

"You think you can insult me like that?" asked the black man. "I'm Louis LaCount. I will remember this insult." Louis turned his back on McGuire. He could feel himself burning with anger. There was nothing he could do. Black men were slaves. He was lucky he was free. But there was war in the wings waiting to happen. The North had people who believed everyone should be free. He, LaCount, believed he would own the world and then, he would pay back that arrogant Southerner. He would get his just deserts very soon from what he had heard. Everyone knew that New Orleans was the capital of wealth, and LaCount had started to get his money and respect from all the people that counted..

LaCount pulled himself together enough to march into the back room. He hated all white Southern men who thought they were gods. They felt the sun rose and set for them. He would find a way some day to make that gambler pay and pay dearly. He loved to think how he would replay him. Something, he wished for and he, LaCount, would use and use again, the men who would kill for pay. He thought of how he would kill that Southern man who thought the world turned for him.

McGuire left the saloon, and found another saloon more to his liking. He played away the night. Watching him play and win was a beautiful black girl. She slide next to him. McGuire patted her fanny for luck. She smiled up to him and blinked her eyes. He could feel himself grow hard and felt the construction of his pants. He turned in his chips and clasped the girl's hand. He knew they had rooms upstairs for the purpose of pleasure. He tugged her hand and she followed him to the steps that led up to the next floor. He was leading her to the stairs when he heard a deep voice saying "Stop."

The girl jumped. She turned. She stared into the cold green eyes of Louis LaCount.

"Go," Louis LaCount said to her, "now."

The girl picked up her skirt and ran away from McGuire. McGuire looked in amazement at this turn of event. "Hey, what do you think you're doing?"

"Making sure you stay away from black people. You're the one who said you had nothing to do with blacks." Louis said as he stood straight and tall.

McGuire walked over to him. "You want to feel my anger? I'm ready to pop you one right now." McGuire picked up his fists and stood ready as any boxer.

Louis picked up his foot, kicked McGuire right in the stomach and walked away.

McGuire fell to the floor, rolled over and got up. He rushed over to Louis and threw a hard punch into Louis's back. Louis stumbled forward. He turned. Louis and McGuire fought till both men were bloody. They kicked and they threw punches, but they were evenly matched. Both were tall and both had the anger to make them strong.

McGuire walked away, as blood dripped from his lips and nose. Louis walked away as bloody. "I'll never forget you," yelled Louis. "You'll be remembered by me forever."

McGuire played in many gambling halls during his stay in New Orleans. His lady Luck was with him every night he gambled. One night he heard Louis LaCount declare someone was cheating. McGuire turned around and looked. There LaCount stood staring at him. His hands flew to his silver guns. He could see LaCount looking at him, and then his eyes turned. He accused another man of cheating. McGuire wanted to kill him there and then, but the crowd looked around coldly. He picked up his winnings and put it in his pocket. He was about to lose this temper, but he held on fast. That LaCount did not accuse him as such, but he felt he was trying to besmirch his character. Never had McGuire been so much as accused of cheating. He was honorable in everything he did. He would never cheat.

McGuire knew it was time to go home when he was accused of cheating. Maybe not accused but intimated that he had. He had his fun but the time was over. He was surprised to learn that the South was fighting the North. Where had he been? He wished he was home so he could fight for the South. It was a no win situation, but it was something he knew he must do. He went to his hotel and packed his bags. To hell with LaCount and all New Orleans, thought McGuire. It was time for his duty to kick in. He left that night on his tall black horse. He had to fight for the South, He had no choice. It was his way of life that they wanted to change. He did not know of any other life to lead except that of the South.

McGuire went home, and joined the Southern Army. His parents wanted him to wait, but wait for what? The South needed him now. He was a plantation owner's son so he was given a commission. He became a Captain over night. The only thing he knew was how to shoot. His family and he and his sister shot since he was a little boy. He led the troops into so many bloody battles. Blood became part of his life. Everything he saw, blood seemed to dampen his being.

Brad McGuire contacted Abe McLeon, his childhood friend and room mate at the University. 'Hey, my friend, I hear you are in the army now. What happened to your ship?" asked McGuire

"Darn it, I lost it during the blockade. It was a miracle that we all came out alive," replied McLeon. "I hate being on land. I love the sea and miss it something awful," said McLeon.

"Wow, and now you're a landlubber. Well, how about us being together, at least we know we can lick the enemy. Or die trying," smiled McGuire

"You think they will let us be together?" asked McLeon

"I don't think they care a whole lot about anything except winning the war," said McGuire.

"I can't think of anyone I want to be with at this time in my life. It is a heck of a war, and I wonder why we are fighting," said McLeon.

"We're fighting because we are Southern. I know of no other reason to fight. My family is of the opinion that we won't be long in winning. That is not how I see it. I think we are in for the long haul. But together we can stand anything. We were roomies at the University, If we can stand each other there, then we can be together again," said McGuire.

"How do I love a good fight." said McLeon ""But better than a good fight by myself, I think being together with you,"

"We'll show those damn Northerners a fight. We can do that and win." smiled Brad McGuire.

"We can fight and fight. Brad, I think the we are too much alike. We always had the same ideas, the same women, and the same do everything we wanted." said McLeon

"Learned to shot and ride together. Went after the same women. We were real rakes." smiled McGuire. "You never settled down, neither did I."

"Not to change the subject, how is your sister doing?" asked McLeon

"I worry about her. She should be in England, near our aunt and uncle. I just don't know what to do." said McGuire. "She's such a flirt, I wonder if she will ever settle down."

"I am in love with your sister," said McLeon

"You stay away from my sister. She's sunshine and innocence. She should be in England with her relatives. She should not be in the states. She needs someone who is gentle and can understand her nature. We are too alike. We like blood and guts. We want fights and laughter. Stay away from my sister. Never go near her." said McGuire

He stared at his friend. Though they were brothers in war, peace and love, McGuire did not want his sister to witness the hardships of life. He wanted her to be merry and happy and to have dreams of innocence.

McLeon shook his head. He understood were McGuire was coming from. They were too much alike to not understand. Though McLeon loved McGuire's sister with a all consuming love forever, he knew he would never be able to give her what she needed. Peace, Happiness, Joy, those things counted in Helen's life.

"I'll stay away as you asked, but I love her with all my heart," said McLeon

"She's not for you," said McGuire.

"I know, I'm just a bad rogue. I'm sorry, but I shall love her all my life," said McLeon

They stared at each other. The hurt was seen in McLean's eyes. They looked at the desolation before them and they were still.

"Who knows if we will live through this," said McGuire. "It is like a world of the unknown. It is death."

"I know this northern lady, she's sort of nice, who might take in your sister," said McLeon. "She's rich and does what she wants. I knew her from when I had a ship to carry her stuff she wanted."

"That would be a relief to my system. Give me her name and I will get it to my sister." said McGuire. "Helen shouldn't be here to see the worst of mankind."

McLeon gave him her name and McGuire felt so much better. He didn't have to worry about his sister. His sister was his worry, and he was glad to send her a letter, telling her to go to this lady. He gathered the information and felt free for once. The war would not hurt his sister. It was a load off his mind, and now he could fight to the death.

McLeon was a fighter, and he never worried about the odds. He was a devil of a fighter. The two units joined together, and they fought side by side. They laughed at the same things and cried about the dead Southern boys. Bombs burst in the air. Boys underage died. Sabers were shinning in the sun and dull in the rain. It rained so much at this time of year. There was so much death in the air. It brought out the worst and the best of the men. They fought and fought.

The fight was tough and the battles were long. Brother against brother. Father against son. Nothing was right, and nothing was wrong. It was a time that should never have happened, but it did. So much for the States rights, so much for other reasons for the war. Men fought and died. Young men who never had a life were burnt like candles before their time. Nothing would be the same again, it was the end of the life they knew and the life they loved. It was over.

Later, they became even better friends during the war. Abe had lost his ship during the blockade and joined the Southern cause just like Brad McGuire. Many a battle was fought by the two men in charge. They had no idea about who was the leader, it just was whoever led first. They became closer than brothers. They were tested in blood. They understood that they would always be close. There was no denying the attractions that they felt for each other. They were brothers in death.

They were taken as prisoners near the end of the conflict. Brad and Abe tried to help the men that were in the jails or just laying on the grass. They watched them die from lack of food or water. They lost many men just from no doctors to take care of their needs. They could turn to no one. Lost in despair, they continued trying to help the men in the prisons. They helped a few, but mostly nothing helped. Brad McGuire became lost in a land of no dimensions. He had nothing to look forward to. Abe McLeon thought only of his ship. He missed the sea. He wanted to sail away from all this misery.

Poor Brad McGuire lost in a no man's land. He wanted nothing, and asked for nothing. All he knew was to get his sister to England, where she would be safe. Then his troubles would end. He would never ask for anything for himself. He misplace his mind to stop his worry.

"The prisoners of the South need help, and no one will give it to them. What are we to do?" asked McGuire

"The best we can. We're lucky that we are strong or we too would be going the way most of the men are going. We are lucky to have each other to depend on." said McLeon. "But what we can do to help is beyond me now. I feel we are lost in a land of no regret."

"We need water, medical help, and food," McGuire shook his head in disbelief that people didn't know this. "What is wrong with the North? Why don't they help us?"

"They are punishing us for thinking of being without them. They hold one union and that is all they think about. They don't care about us, as individuals," said McLeon.

"We will die. All of us will die," said McGuire.

"No, we'll live to tell the tale to our children, and they will tell their children, and so the war will live forever," said McLeon

"True," said McGuire as he sank into the dirt that encircled the fort were they lay. The rags of their clothing encased their bodies, but they still laughed and cried together.

The two men needed food and water, but they gave short shift to their desires. They cared for the men around them. They were leaders, and lead they would by any means they could.

The end of the war came faster than either man thought. It was over, and the North was the victor. The prisoners were freed to return to their homes, or what was left of their homes. With no where to go, men wandered the land, lost and betrayed. Carpet baggers came and the world was harsh to the South. How dare the South want to leave the union?

The end of the war and there were no more Southern mansions, no more Southern plantations, and no more money to buy anything. The South was on their knees without even a tin cup to put out for hand outs. There was no going back to the old life. McLeon left to find a ship to cross the Atlantic. He was desperate for a ship again. He was a sailor and not a land person. McGuire found himself with an empty heart and mind. He missed his friend, brother, or whatever they had become in the long war. Brad only knew how to gamble. He had no trade. At least McLeon had a ship to go back to, but Brad McGuire had nothing of any value. McGuire had no one to tell his troubles to, as all his family had left this earth in death, and his sister, whom he loved, had to be send to England. She had to be safe. He wanted the best for her. He did not want her to know how bad the things had occurred in the South.

He finally got enough money, so that he could send his sister, Helen, to England and to his aunt. His Aunt Rose was his mother's sister. He felt as if he won the best horse race in town to have his sister go to England. His responsibility to his family was over once his sister left. He had no one to care for now. He just was going to roll around the United States. He had nothing to show for all the years his family had owned the plantation. He had nothing. Yet, he felt like a emperor having the money to send Helen off in all innocence. He wanted her to laugh and sing. He wanted her to be a ray of sunshine always. He loved his sister.

He had ended up in Cactus Gulch when his uncle had left him a saloon, a hotel and a whore house. He knew nothing about running those establishments. Therefore, having a gambling nature, when he was jilted by his true love, he gave it all away. He felt you win some, you lose some, and he surely lost. He started traveling again looking for something he had a compulsion to find. He knew he would never find his true love, - Samantha. The fairy princess he had dreamed about but could never possess

He still thought about it every day. He had saved her from mud, cleaned her school house, and taken her virginity. Even so, she did not want to marry him. So he roamed and roamed and finally ended up in New Orleans. He had not forgotten the fact that he had made a fatal enemy of Louis LaCount. In case in point, he just never thought about that man until now as he roamed this wilderness next to the river. The black man had meant nothing to him then or when he came into New Orleans. Then he found out how the world really turns and how hatred could last forever. He remembered the lady in the river that he had saved. To throw someone into the churning water was death.

He just didn't want or know of any enemies. He just played cards and felt his life drifting away life the river. Heck, he just wanted nothing to think about. Then the letter came that his sister was coming back to live with him. Why in the world would she want to live with him? He just had to reform, or something like get her married or -. Well, what was he to do? That was why he was on the river in the first place. In the second place, why didn't he mind his own business and not jump into the river and save that woman. Third, why was he where he saw the lady thrown into the river, was it fate?

Then he remembered why he got LaCount so angry with him.

McGuire came into New Orleans, he had gold, that he had hidden, back on the plantation. His friend held close to his heart remained his lover, Lady Luck. That was all he had. He swore he would have nothing to do with any woman. He was tired of a loveless life. He wanted a woman who would really love him. So he didn't care if he had money or not as he supported no woman. Just enough to eat and have a place to sleep remained all he wanted.

When he went into the Parrot Saloon, he felt he was going to win. His lady was with him. He could feel her. So he sat down at the poker table and started to play. He played for about four hours. He was winning quite a great amount of money.

"Cheater, cheater. Watch how he cheats." came the cool voice he remembered some where in the back of his mind.

McGuire looked up and stared into the cold green eyes of Louis LaCount. McGuire pushed back from the table. His hands went to his silver guns. McQuire's lake blue eyes looked like ice.

"I never cheated in my life," snarled McGuire. "Who you calling a cheater?" McGuire looked into the cold green eyes of LaCount.

LaCount looked at McGuire. He saw McQuire's hands on his silver guns. He saw the lake-blue eyes cold with death. For the first time in his life, LaCount could see that living or dying did not mean anything to McGuire. LaCount had counted on the fact that everyone wanted to live, but McGuire just didn't give a damn.

LaCount smiled with his mouth. "Sorry, wasn't talking to you." LaCount and McGuire looked at each other. They felt the hatred run through their bodies. They would get even one way or another. LaCount walked away, and McGuire pushed his chips up. He piled them in his hands and brought them over to the cashier. So, LaCount changed his mind about cheaters. McGuire could shoot an eagle out of the sky, and he just didn't care if he lived or died.

McGuire felt a chill around his shoulders and down his back. Yeah, he was going to have to watch his back from now on. That LaCount was going to do something dirty. He knew this was a day his luck was running away from him. It was the same day, that he received the letter that his sister was coming to New Orleans to be with him. To meet her to travel down the river with her. God, how much worse luck can a man have.

He pushed his hands into his pockets of his pants. When Lady Luck turned sour, there was just nothing to do but hope for the best that She would come back to him.

His sister coming to New Orleans was the last thing he ever thought would happen. What was he going to do with her around? His sister, Helen, was so innocent with her golden hair and her lake-blue eyes, she wasn't safe here from any man. He had hoped she would marry and stay in England. Why did she come back to the States? He wanted to ask, but was afraid, as her eyes were so sad. What could have happened in so short a time?

He turned his back, and in front of him stood the bartender. He held a shot gun in his hands. The boom of the gun exploded around his head. He looked around, and there lay a bushwhacker. Dead, against the railing. He stared at the bartender, and smiled. His Lady Luck was with him still.

Chapter V

CLAIRESE PACED BACK AND FORTH. First he wanted her then he didn't make love to her. All men wanted her body, she thought. Here she was in just a chemise and pantaloons and now he acted as if she was wearing armor. She pulled her hand through her stone colored hair. It was tangled and she must look a mess, but she knew she had a great body. Even LaCount had loved her body.

"Why don't you make love to me again?" shouted Clairese "You did it last night.".

McGuire looked at her without any emotion. "I beg your pardon. I really think I did quite enough for you. Like saving your sorry ass".

"Look," cried Clairese, "I'm really a good lay. I bet you never had anyone like me before. Why don't you want more? What is wrong with you?"

"I don't want to get involved in any woman. In case you haven't noticed, you are a woman," said McGuire as he kicked the mud with his bare feet.

McGuire walked over to her and handed her a clam on a shell. She looked down at the clam. She shrugged her shoulders making sure her breast were swaying as she shrugged. She blinked her eyes, and her long black lashes swept down and then up. She stared at McGuire with a sultry look.

They stood that way for a second. McGuire said, "Eat"

Clairese slumped down onto the ground. She examined the clam like she never wanted to eat some thing that ugly. She looked up at McGuire. He had turned away from her. She felt like she was a weed in a garden, but one that even the gardener overlooked. What was wrong with her? She wanted McGuire with all her heart. She looked at the light shinning on the golden hair of McGuire. She felt the first frenzy of desire. Her stomach churned in need.

She turned around to look at him fully. Nothing. He was not looking at her. She wanted to spread her legs and invite him in. But he just didn't look at her with any desire. LaCount always wanted her, morning, noon and night. That was true, until he got tired of her. Too much of a good thing, she thought.

McGuire stared at the waters of the Mississippi. His brain was confused with the ideas that floated by, like the debris that floated on the waters. What a fool he was. He should have seen it clearly before now. He and Clairese were sitting ducks. For sure, LaCount had sent men to be sure they never got to New Orleans. What better way then just kill them along the river and they would never be heard from again.

People would think that they drowned. But what about his sister, Helen? What would become of her? She could not survive on her own. She was hot house breed. He pounded his fist into his other hand. He had to get to New Orleans. He had to be sure his sister was back in England, no matter what she wanted. He could not think of why she came back to the states. She was safe in England, and that was were she must go.

Helen, the sweet dear girl, who did not know the terrible things done to women when they are alone. He had to take steps, and he had to take them now. All Clarese could think of was sex. Well, he would wake her up. Plus, as he said before, the hell with sex. He -well- he just had to get to New Orleans no matter what to help his sister. After that, well, he sure wasn't going to play games with any woman any more. A bachelors life for him, is what he thought, a life without women to haunt him and bother him.

McGuire turned to Clarese. She had been sitting under a tree eating a turtle he had cooked. First a clam he had cooked and then a turtle. McGuire cursed himself. Fires leave trails, what had he been thinking. No more cooking, no more flirting, no more leaving tracks in the mud. He had to think as if he was in the Southern army. He had to be brave and worry what the enemy would do.

"Get up Clairese, and stopped stuffing your big mouth. We have to go into the woods and then talk." McGuire said as he pulled Clairese up from the ground.

Clairese shrugged off his hands. Maybe he came to his senses and wanted some sex. Then she looked at his face. It was stone cold. She started to yell at him, but he quickly put his large hands over her mouth. "For gods sake, shut up and listen. Or do you want to be dead?"

Clairese looked at him with startled eyes. Her large black-gray eyes bulged.

"Will you be quiet and listen?" asked McGuire

Clairese nodded her head. Her small hands hugged her waist as she looked at McGuire as if he had lost his mind.

McGuire pulled her into the wooded area. Clairese looked around for snakes, or maybe a bear.

"LaCount, will be looking for us. He wants us both dead. You know that. I know that, and yet we act like a couple of kids on an outing. We never even gave a thought about him. Well, we better. I bet he has men looking for us on both sides of the river."

Clairese looked at him with her big black-gray eyes. Her long black lashes swept up and down as she nodded her head. "Yeah, we should think about that snake, LaCount. He wants me dead. Do you know why? Well, I'll tell you now, straight off. I caught him cheating on me. That is when I went up river.

I hired someone to kill him. I don't have the nerve to do it. But I went up river and found me a man who would be willing to kill that monster. You know he was going forget about me, and be through with me. After all the years I have given him. Did he think I was a towel to throw away and not care what happened to it? Well, they found out what I did. That's why they threw me in the water, and killed the man I hired."

Clairese let the tears fall from her big black-gray eyes. "I loved that man. I really did. But he just used me for whatever he wanted. I was content, just as long as he loved me, or at least let me love him. God he is a monster."

Clairese threw herself into McQuire's chest. McQuire's arms went around Clarisse's body. He held her tightly. What did he know? He couldn't help himself. He loved the ladies. He clucked and smoothed Clarisse's back.

"Sh, sh. It will be OK." said McGuire as he looked down at her golden honey skin. "We'll get back to New Orleans. We'll be fine. Just have to be careful from now on."

Clairese just let the tears fall from her eyes. "You don't know what it is like to love someone and they don't love you. You just don't know how the heart hurts. I tried to have you love me, just to see if that would help. But the truth is, nothing can help when you love someone so much. I hope you never know. "Clarisse shut her mouth as she did not want McGuire to know it was him she was in love with. He was her golden angel.

McGuire let go of Clairese. He took her face in his hands. He looked deeply into her eyes. "I knew you just wanted someone to make love to you so you would forget LaCount. I'm no wind up action figure as there is nothing left in me to make love to someone. I loved, I lost. That is what is wrong with me. You think you're the only one who had a love? I loved Samantha with all my heart and soul. She threw it all into my face. She married a rancher. Yeah, a real honest to goodness rancher. Can you believe that?"

McGuire slid on to the ground. He sat there as though there was no tomorrow. "I had a hotel, a whore house I was willing to give up and a saloon. And she choose a rancher. To work on a ranch. Hard Work. Hard Work. She would work on a ranch then be married to me. I had plenty of money then. But the truth of the matter was, I didn't know I loved her until she threw me over for anther man. Then it broke my heart."

McGuire rocked back and forth where he sat. He felt like he was a kid again and wanted to cry for the unfairness of life. He stared at the ground. Then his eyes swept up to Clairese. She stood in her underclothes shivering. The night was coming on and the days were getting colder.

"I'm sorry," Clairese said, as she sat down besides McGuire. "I didn't know you loved and lost. Why go to New Orleans. Let's make tracks to the West and leave this rotten place. Why go back. Why are we going back?"

McGuire looked at Clairese long and hard. "I have to go back. My sister, Helen is there. I have to make sure she is alright. I have to send her back to England. Why the hell she came to New Orleans I don't know. If she didn't come, I would never have been on that river boat. I never would have jumped into the water to save you. We would not be here hoping to get to New Orleans before they kill us."

Clairese stared at McGuire, "I could go West by myself then. I have no future in New Orleans."

"Look, do what you want Clairese. I'm going back to New Orleans. In a box or alive, but I am going back. I have a sister to worry about. I don't need to worry if you want to go or not. I am not forcing you to do anything. You understand. Just do your own thing."

Standing up and patting her clothing for dirt, Clairese looked at McGuire. "So, we go to New Orleans. Truth, I can't make this on my own. You know that. Guess we better start looking to cover our tracks. I bet he sent his best trackers out after us. We don't stand a chance in hell if he did."

McGuire laughed. A slow soft laugh escaped his mouth. "Clairese, I have to tell you, I have been in the war, and I have been out West. I think we can make it if we are careful. I really do."

Looking around the mud they had tramped on, McGuire walked back to the mud. He tracked his footsteps to the river. Then he moved very carefully back using his foot steps to walk backwards to the trees. He made Clairese do the same. It took a long time for them to accomplish this. But it looked like they had gone into the river. He then climbed a tree and helped Clairese up the tree. He crawled as far as he could out on a limb, and grabbed the limb of the next tree. He carefully swung over to the next tree.

Without talking Clairese did the same. She crawled out on the limb. McGuire put out his hand and grabbed her. He swung her over to the next tree where he was laying on the tree limb. Slowly they moved from tree to tree in this slow fashion, until the night shut the light from the sky.

"McGuire," whispered Clairese, "I am so afraid."

"Call me Brad," McGuire whispered back

"Brad. It is such a nice name for a wonderful man." said Clairese

"Thanks," said McGuire

"LaCount use to buy me red dresses. Oh, such a great many red dresses. I loved the man. I really did. I could not believe he would ever throw me away," lamented Clairese. "He thought I looked fetching in red."

"I think I am going crazy with want of food. I find you so amazing. I think I am falling in love with you," said McGuire

"With me?" Clairese said in wonder. "I have loved you since you rescued me. I thought you would never notice me. I thought - well, never mind. Brad, tell me more about you," said Clairese

"Let me hear about your red dresses," said McGuire

"LaCount said I looked so extremely beautiful in red. Once in awhile he let me wear bright yellow. I never had anyone but him. I didn't know of anyone but him. He held my heart forever. I could not believe he would get rid of me. Me! But then the cold water the Mississippi, showed me what he thought of me," said Clairese

"How did you find out? About his throwing you away. You know, how did you feel? What did you do?" asked McGuire

"I found out by accident. Don't all facts fall on accidents. Any way, he found a new lady to love. She was almost white. Not like me," said Clairese. "I was walking on the grounds one day, and there he was with this almost white woman. He was telling her how much he loved her, and how he would get rid of me. I could not believe he said that," cried Clairese

"What did you do?" asked McGuire.

"I said I had to go North because of my mother. I never did know my mother, but I had to hire a man to kill LaCount. How he found out I do not know, But he knows every thing that goes on. Probably he knew I never knew my mother," Clairese wiped her eyes with her fingers.

"Bummer," said McGuire.

"Did you mean it, that you feel you are falling in love with me?" asked Clairese

"Yes. I guess it is lack of food, or the mud, or maybe being close to you. I just don't know what. But you look better and better to me." said McGuire

"But I'm half black, and you're a Southerner. How can you love me?" asked Clairese.

"I told you, I don't know. You just looked good to me. We can go West and start a horse training program. We can marry. I don't know," replied McGuire

"I can't believe you think you might love me. I'm over whelmed by the compliment. Think about it long and hard. I shall treasure it forever. I never had a man tell me he might love me," Clairese shook her body and hugged herself.

On a big old tree, McGuire and Clairese huddled close together to keep warm. They tried to stretch out but they were afraid of falling off the tree. "We have to take turns sleeping." whispered McGuire. "You go first, I'll wake you in a few hours, and you can make sure I don't fall off this limb."

Clairese was about to whisper back when they heard a sound reverberate through the trees. Something was coming. It was close. They shivered in anticipation; Was it the trackers or a wild animal.

They looked at each other, and something passed in their eyes. They knew that they would be together no matter what happened to them. They were bonded in love or what ever that lay between then.

Chapter VI

HELEN LAY IN BED AND stared at the white curtains. That was it, she thought, she was white and he was black. If she turned black he would not want her. She had to make herself into a black woman. How can she to do that?

She sat up in bed and stared at her suitcases. The brown shoe polish! She would apply it to her arms and then her breasts. How was she going to get it on her back? She would think of something. Then her hair. Well, she would rinse it in shoe polish.

She scrubbed the shoe polish on her hands and arms. Then she applied it to her breasts. She was glowing with energy, when the door flew open and Louis LaCount stood at the open door. He looked at her with his cold green eyes.

He was dressed all in white, jacket, vest, shirt, ascot, pants. For a slit second, all was still. Then LaCount roared, "Mrs. Smithy, come here and bring a tub and lots of hot water now."

Helen slipped her wrapper on her shoulders. She felt the chill of LaCount's eyes on her. She wanted to hide and scream at the same time. She did not know what to do.

"What are you doing?" He strode over to her bed where she sat. He yanked at her arm. "You know already that you belong to me?" he asked. "I brought you a dress. You should always wear white. You are like a star, shiny and bright. I have many dresses made for you."

Mrs. Smithy came running with her helpers of two girls carrying pails of hot water. Mrs. Smithy seemed like she came out of her bed all pulled together in the wrong way. The women dumped the water into the tub. LaCount took off his jacket and vest. He stared at Helen. He unbuttoned his shirt and ascot, He made sure the diamond stick pin was laid carefully on the dresser. He watched as the women filled the tub. He took off his pants and stood there naked with his shiny black skin blurred by the all white room.

He walked slowly over to Helen's bed. She looked at him with hate and tear filled eyes. He took her hand and pulled the wrapper from her body. She was now as naked as he was. She tried to bring the blanket up over her body, but he held her hands and kept them against her body. He picked her up in his arms and carried her to the tub. He threw her into the water. The steam scolded Helen's body. She felt the heat on her skin and wanted to scream. She could see no mercy in his eyes. She closed her mouth as tears streamed down her face.

He held her loosely as he looked his fill on his possession. She was his and there was no way out for her. He knew his power and he would use it. As far as her brother was concerned, he would make sure he was dead and buried. It was Helen he wanted and would have. The brother was a fly in his life. It did not matter to him, only Helen mattered.

He scrubbed her arms and hands. Then he gently scrubbed her breasts. "If I didn't know better, I would think you lost your mind." Louis said as he looked into her eyes.

"Do not touch me," screamed Helen. "No black man should see me naked. Leave me be."

"You are talking to the man who you are going to marry. I am not use to women who do not want me. You will change your mind, or I will change your mind. It does not matter which."

"I will not eat with you. I will not do anything with you. Let me out of this tub." screamed Helen as she swirled her body around in the tub.

Louise just laughed as he held her head in his hands and patted her hair. It was so golden. He had never dreamed of hair this color. Yes, he had seen it on her brother, but on her it was like the first sunshine he had ever seen. He pulled the pins from her hair and it uncoiled down her back and around her body. It was like a veil of silk floating in the water. He bent down and kissed her breast. Then he kissed the other breast and he could see her face as she felt the heat of the kiss. He pulled her closer to his body His penis stood thick and ready. He let his hand run down Helen's leg. Then he closed his hand over her other leg until it reached where they joined. He let his fingers reach into her hidden place. He watched her face. She was like a child as the heat of her body spread over her love place. He watched as she tried to hide her distress and her want of something she knew not what.

"You want me," stated LaCount. "I have planned something for you and me. I shall not change my plans now, even though I could take you as I should. There is nothing holding me back except this is not what I planned."

He took her out of the tub and wrapped her in a large towel. He held her closely. Then his mouth took her mouth in to his and he kissed her, with passion that drew her soul into her throat. She could not believe this was happening to her. She tried to move, but the large towel wrapped around her felt like a cocoon. He held her tightly and looked into her eyes. He could see the fear that flashed in her eyes. He laughed. It was exactly what he wanted.

Helen looked in the mirror, she was white again. He pulled the towel away from her, and she stood naked as she looked into the mirror. Her hair was like a veil as it surrounded her body. Why was he here so early? What could she do to stop him? She had said she would eat with LaCount yesterday. But really, how could she eat with a man that was black. After all, she came from the South and- -She turned away from the mirror and pulled on her petticoats. She tied them around her waist and patted the pure white muslin down as she thought. What was she doing saying she would eat with that man?

He gave her the dress he had brought. She looked at it. It was the latest fashion and it was new. It was so very white the dress, embroidered with yellow flowers. He placed his hands on the small buttons down the back. He shook the dress until it danced in his hands. "This is what you should wear tonight. It is exactly what I would dream of you wearing. It is what you shall always wear, white. Pure simple white."

Helen looked at the dress as if it was the evil of the world. He held the dress ready for her to step into it. "Wear it" he said. "You will do as I say, I expect it. You are all alone in this world. I am looking for your brother as you wish, but don't make me angry. I want you."

Helen shook as she stood with her petticoats around her waist. She looked down at the rug and thought of her brother. She did want LaCount to find her brother. But would her brother help her now?

She stepped into her dress. It was white organize with yellow roses embroidered around the waist and hem. She tried to button the back of the dress herself, but it was almost impossible. She should have worn some thing she had in her own trunk. Now she looked at herself in the mirror, the dress hanging from her shoulders. She could hear LaCount laugh. He was having fun with her and her buttons. She moved her eyes up and looked at his cold green eyes.

"I think you need my help. In fact, I think you will need my help forever. That is how long I shall keep you." said LaCount

Her hair was golden curls circling her face. Her large lake-blue eyes stared back into his cold green eyes. She seemed to be in a trance as she looked at him. She didn't know what to think or do.

"I - I want you to find my brother. I need you to find my brother. I just don't know what to do now," Helen said as she stared into his eyes.

"Then be good to me," smiled LaCount

She was about to take the dress off as she could not think of anything else to do, when she felt his hands on her back. He was buttoning the buttons of the dress. She could feel his fingers on her skin. She wanted to slap his face, but was so afraid he might not find Brad, her brother for her. LaCount was standing there in front of her, and his hands encircled her body as he buttoned her dress. She gasped as she looked at him. She knew he wore white to make sure she saw how black he was. His pride showed in his blackness.

He smiled at her as he noticed her lake-blue eyes blinking. "Are you ready to eat? I thought we should had a cocktail first. Would that please you?"

"I, I think I'm not up to going out right now. I think I shall just stay here in the room tonight." Helen said as she tried to face him. She heard him laugh. He was enjoying himself at her expense.

"Why Miss Helen, you are only half dressed. You need a maid. I can tell you don't know how to dress yourself. Look at you. Not every button in your back is buttoned. Except the few buttons I closed. "

Helen's face turned red. "How do you know I haven't buttoned my back? Maybe that is how I like it."

"I can see your dress is open in the mirror.," he laughed.

Helen looked down to the rug. She did not know what to say to this man. If only Brad was here to protect her. She was so alone. The only person who seemed to care about her was this man, LaCount. But he was black, and she was told to never trust a black man. Yet, he had held her in the bath tub and she felt the odd tingles of her heart.

He moved up to her and putting his hands on her shoulders, he turned her around. "I guess I shall button you all the way this time. I'll send you a maid for the future. You know you cannot do any thing yourself. You were brought up to be waited on. My dear, no one expects you to do anything for yourself. I expect you to be the perfect wife to me."

He took the first button in his hand and looked at her milk white flesh. He touched her back. Helen jumped. "Hold still," LaCount said, "I'm only buttoning your dress. When I want more, I will take it."

Helen shivered as he continued to button her dress. He turned her around and looked into her face. Helen took a step back and bumped into the bed. He followed her step and stood close to her. His face came down close to her face. She wanted to scream.

"You afraid of a black man?" said LaCount. "afraid I'll rape you?"

"No, No, I'm -" Helen stopped as tears filled her eyes.

LaCount pulled her close to his body and kissed her full on her lips. She tried to step back and fell across the bed. LaCount followed suit and lay on top of her. He laid his hands on her breasts. He looked into her eyes. She closed her eyes. She was so afraid. LaCount rose from the bed and started to dress himself. "A very difficult exercise in will power" he said as he laughed. "I want you, but it will wait."

"Look at me," LaCount said in a soft voice. "You are going to marry me. Yes, me, a black man. How about that?: And you will be mistress to my mansion "River Walk." You will have servants and pretty clothes. Jewels you never even dreamed about, and all this, because I want you to be mine. Do you understand? I want some one with the knowledge of the rich and the spoiled. That's you of course. Somehow or other, you have wormed your way into my heart. I truly did not think I had a heart, but I saw you on the River boat, and my breathing stopped. You were the woman I have dreamed about forever, but thought I would never actually see."

LaCount pulled her face closer with one hand, while the

other hand played with her breasts. He kissed her long and hard. She opened her mouth to scream and he stuck his tongue into her mouth with a back and forth motion. She lay still, stunned. No man had ever stuck his tongue into her mouth. It was such an odd sensation. She lost control of herself.

LaCount stood up and let his fingers sort out any creases in his suit. He held out his hand and Helen just looked at it. He grabbed one of her slim hands and pulled her up.

"You'll get use to me." smiled LaCount. "Let us go down stairs and get in my carriage and we will go and eat at the Court of Love. It is a special place and made for special people, Like us."

LaCount went to the door, and brought in a cape. He put it around her as he kissed her ear and then her neck. Like a stone statue, Helen stood and could not breathe. She knew that she was in trouble. Bad trouble. She felt her body tremble.

"I thought you might need a cape as it is chilly out. I didn't think you just wanted to go to eat in just a dress. Of course, we shall have you in jewels and furs." said LaCount.

LaCount stepped away from her back and put his arm out for her to take hold of his arm. He looked as if he was going to laugh at her. He took her slim hand in his and put it through his arm. Then he opened the door. LaCount thought of his life with Helen. He would have this beautiful wife who would obey his every wish. Plus he would get even with McGuire but it was not what he wanted. He wanted Helen, and Helen alone. He had promised himself he would take something McGuire loved and treasured and he would use it again and again. He did not want to use McGuire and his hatred. He wanted only to be with Helen. He felt his heart lurch in his chest. He wanted her any way he could have her. He would use Helen forever. She was meant for him.

"I have special meal planned for us. I am sure you will love it." LaCount said as he swept her down into his carriage. He felt the eyes of her land lady looking at them. So let her look. White trash was what she was. He knew what he wanted, and he knew how to get what he wanted. He wanted Helen as his wife, and the mistress of his mansion. She knew all about mansions, and plantations. That was her world. Why she can't even dress without a maid. He watched her closely and could see she was use to maids and servants. She knew exactly what to tell them to do, and would see that they obeyed what orders she gave. She would give him beautiful children.

He looked at her heaving breasts. He thought of white snow with a pink cherry on top. He would eat it. His black skin would only make her skin look whiter. She was so pale right now. He knew she was frightened, but that was what he wanted her to be. She was going to be his woman, and nothing was going to stop that from happening. Her brother would be dead and she was his and his alone.

He placed her in the carriage with the large gold letters she had noticed at the dock. She wanted to huddle in the seat, but LaCount pulled her towards him as he seated himself.

"Are you comfortable?" asked LaCount.

Helen wanted to scream, cry, almost anything, except answer him. She was so afraid of him. "I'm very comfortable."

"Good. You will get use to my touching you. You like it. I can see it in your eyes. Yes, you like it. You do not know what you feel right now, but you will love me as I expect you to." said LaCount with conviction.

Helen did not know if he was right. Did she feel different about him? Was she feeling less afraid? She let him touch her. She felt his hands wandering around her busts. She could feel him squeeze her right bust. Then he went to her left bust. She sat there feeling his hands grasp her and she felt her blood churn within her body. He touched her and she did not fight back.

The carriage had two men on the back as it rattled and moaned. The carriage and the horses rushed through the cobble stone street. The houses all went to the street with wrought iron balconies fronting the windows that reminded one of the gay nights of Paris. Finally, in a dark alley, the carriage stopped. The carriage door was opened by one of the attendants that stood in the back of the carriage. LaCount got out and took Helen's hand. He gently steered her out of the carriage. He noted her small foot as she exited the carriage. God, he was mad about this woman. Nothing in his life felt like this. His body screamed for her to be nearer. He could rape her right where they stood. He would wait. The time had to be right, she was to be his wife, not his mistress.

"Come," said LaCount as he led her up a flight of white steps. The door flew open. The man who opened the door was a small white man. He had red hair and big ears. He bowed low as LaCount strode by him holding Helen firmly in his hand.

"I think we shall have a drink on the terrace first," LaCount said as he led her along a long hall. "By the way, this is one of my houses. Do you like it? I use it for my mistresses. Do you think I should keep my mistresses once we are married? But then, I guess we shall see what I shall do. You will be happy as you are use to servants."

Helen's eyes grew wide as she was hustled down the long hall. They entered a room that had sofas, and chairs, and a large glass door. LaCount opened the door and they were on a terrace filled with the smell of honeysuckle. LaCount pulled a chair from the wrought iron table and motioned Helen to sit.

"There is no choice but to sit for awhile. I want this to be perfect. I want you to see me as a man, not as a color." said LaCount.

The metal of the chair engulfed her, as Helen sat down. She watched LaCount out of the corner of her eye. Her cape covered her dress. What was wrong with her?

A tall black butler entered with a tray of drinks and some food to nibble on. He set the tray down and handed the first drink to Helen. She looked at it. She did not recognize the drink. The waiter put the small plates filled with fried shrimp and fried oysters on the table. He handed LaCount his drink and left.

LaCount looked at Helen. The light of the moon shone on her golden hair. She looked like an angel who had come to earth. "The drink is bourbon. Just bourbon. So drink up."

"I never drink," said Helen as she put the glass back on the tray.

"Pick up the drink, and drink it," Louis LaCount said with a laugh.

LaCount took a big swallow and watched Helen. She put the glass to her lips and tried to sip the bourbon. She made an ugly face as it slid down her throat. "You'll get use to it. It is my drink. You know, you have to like what I like. Do you have any Questions you want to ask me?"

Helen looked at him with empty eyes. She was washed out. Frozen in time. Then she felt life return to her body. She thought of her brother, Brad.

"My brother, what about my brother. What has happened to him?" Helen whimpered

"Oh, didn't I tell you. I sent trackers down both sides of the river to see if they can find him. I knew you wanted to know if he was alive or dead." LaCount said as he put his hand on top of her slim white hand.

As she pulled her hand away, LaCount grabbed her hand and held it tightly. "What's the matter Miss Helen? Can't stand to see the black and white together. Think of what our children will look like. Do you think they will be black, white, or mixed?"

Tears streamed down Helen's face. She stared at LaCount and felt her world turn around in a mix of colors. "I don't want to marry you."

"Strange, but you will. You have very little choice. What if your brother is dead? What will you do? Will you work for a living? Doing what? All you can do is lay down and be a whore.

Is that your ambition? I can give you everything you are use to having. I can add the extras of jewelry and furs. I can give you a mansion which is like the one you grew up in. What do you want Miss Helen?"

Helen sat in a daze. She did not want a black man, but she wanted her brother. Only LaCount could find him. Only LaCount would know that she was all alone.

"Here let me pour you another drink," said LaCount

"I can feel the first drink already," Helen said as she tried to shake her head.

Louis LaCount took her hand and placed it on her mouth. "Drink" He said.

"The world in spinning, I feel so strange." cried Helen

LaCount looked at her with his strange eyes. He put his arms around her body. She stood up and swayed. He groped for her body. He felt her lean away, and then she stopped. "There are two of you. Two black men, It can not be." Helen pulled her body away and sat down again on the chair.

Wiping her eyes with her small handkerchief, Helen just looked at LaCount. LaCount stood up. "Time to eat. I bet your hungry. I can see it in your eyes. Your land lady said you had nothing to eat all day. Is that because you have no money to pay her. I can remedy that, of course I will. You must never go hungry again. You are to be the wife of LaCount. I am a very famous man here in New Orleans. I own almost everything and every body."

Helen looked at his green eyes. She drowned in his eyes. Her head whirled around her. She counted two, no three black men. Was she awake or asleep?

Taking her arm, LaCount raised her from her seat. She could smell his odor of spice and leather, heat and lust. She wanted to hide, or maybe, even kill herself. She could not let that man touch her again. Where was he taking her? There were too many black men now. She could never hide from them all.

He looked at her pale face and slender body. He who hated

all white Southerners with a passion; He was lost in a dream of love and lust. He stared at her. He would have her this very night. Nothing in the world would stop that from happening. He had held himself back for too long. He wanted her and he was going to have her.

He led her into the house and out of the room they had entered to go to the terrace. He turned a corner and there in front of them was a dining room which looked like it was set in England. Helen gasped as she looked. The polished wood of the dinning room table gleamed in the candle light. The large upholstered chairs stretched out. The table was about ten feet long..

Only one corner of the table was filled with silverware. The head of the table and the seat to the right of the head. LaCount seated her at his right and then seated himself. Smiling at her, he rang a little bell. The waiter came in carrying turtle soup. He ladled out. the soup into their bowls. Then he left, and came back again carrying a tray filled with different breads.

"You must be starved," said LaCount. "You must not ever be hungry again. In fact, I think you will stay here tonight. I do not want you to leave. I want you here where I see you, hear you, and breath you."

Helen looked at LaCount, but her eyes wandered to his green eyes. She could not help herself. Then she heard what he said. She would not stay here. She would leave. He could not stop her.

Helen's eyes darted to the bread. She could take it home and eat the next day. How could she do it? Maybe draw his attention to something else.

LaCount laughed. "So, you are hungry. Don't worry, my dear. I shall see to it that you have breakfast and lunch. I really care about you."

Picking up her spoon, Helen looked at LaCount. He was going to do with her as he wanted. Something told her she could not escape. What had happened to her life. She should have stayed in England. But then- She took a sip of the soup. It was delicious. She was so hungry. She wanted to pick up the bowl and just drink it all down. But manners were always necessary. So she spooned the soup slowly into her mouth.

"Would you like an engagement party first? Yes, of course you do. What am I thinking. We shall have the party next week. Will that suit you? Of course it will." LaCount took a spoon of soup into his mouth. He wanted to laugh out loud. Helen was his to do as he liked. He knew she was defeated. She will gladly become his wife. Much preferred than a mistress as she was high class, and knew all the right situations with the touch of the rich. One had to be bred to wealth to understand what to do. No common woman could be like Helen, a mistress of the old plantation . .

So he opened his mouth into a smile. "My dear, do not tell me you would rather be my mistress. If so, this would be the house you would live in. But really, I do not think you are they type to be a mistress, when you can be mistress of a mansion. And of course, my wife."

LaCount leaned close to her. "Tell me, what do you want? To be my mistress or my wife?"

"I want to go home," cried Helen. "I want to go home."

"So where is your home, Miss Helen? Where should I take you?" snarled LaCount

Helen put down her spoon. She looked at the white tablecloth. She shifted the silverware in front of her. Then she turned her huge lake-blue eye on LaCount. "I can never love you. I can never marry a man of color. I can not in truth want anything from you."

"Oh Helen, you are such a liar. How will you survive if I do not help you. You know that is true. You know I am the only one you can count on. You know that you will marry me, as you have no choice. You will learn to love me, and if you don't why I shall teach you how you will love me, even if it means beating you to death."

LaCount stood up and pulled Helen from her chair. He crushed her to his body. He held her in his strong hands. His face came down and kissed her with heat and passion. He pulled her closer and she could feel his manhood against her body. His large hands grasped her backside. She was pulled closer to his body so that his manhood pushed against her stomach.

She twisted away from him. Out the room and down the hall, she ran. She ran to the door they had entered. She opened the door and fled to the steps. She ran outside to the steps. She started down the steps and his hand grasped her around her waist. She turned and scratched his hand. She fought with all her might. She would not let a black man touch her. He pulled her to his body. She tried the steps, but all she found was empty space. The steps were too far away.

He pulled her to his body and he knew he was in heaven. It was so good to have her close. His heart, that he swore he did not have, pounded. His sensations spread into his soul. He was going to have this lady for life. It was something his feelings told him.

He grabbed her and carried her inside. He looked at her with fire in his heart.

"I will have you, now." he croaked. He pulled at her dress.

Suddenly, the buttons on her dress popped open as he pulled the dress down. He leaned further down and pulled her chemise off her shoulders and her snow white breasts were bare. He looked at her small pink nipples. Just as he dreamed and what he had seen in the wash tub. He put his mouth on her breast and suckled. He turned his face up to hers. He pulled her down to the floor. He ripped the dress from her body, and then he ripped off each petticoat.

The firelight played on her white skin. He looked at her laying on the rug. He picked her up and carried her out of the room into his bedroom. He laid her on his bed. Tears escaped

Helen's eyes. She could not believe what was happening to her. LaCount looked at her naked body. He could see the moonlight coming into the room slanting across her body.

"Please, no, please, no." cried Helen

LaCount pulled off his shirt and jacket and pulled off his boots. He ripped off his pants. He could not wait another moment in time. He stared at Helen. He had never seen a woman as beautiful as she. He could taste her like an exquisite cream. He lay on the side of her. "Don't cry, my love. It will be alright, we are going to marry. I want you. I have to have you now."

Helen's face turned red and then white. She understood; she did not know what LaCount would do next. Her outlook was at a stand still.

LaCount took her in his arms and his fingers floated around her body. His kisses covered every inch of her body. He pulled her closer. He sucked again on her breast as his hand fondled her secret place. Then he raised above her and pushed himself into her body. She screamed, and fainted. He was her first. Blood came from her body as he watched it spread into the sheets. He could not believe his luck. He was the first to have her.

LaCount pulled himself out of her body. He looked down on her. He slid off the bed and brought a handkerchief soaked in water. He bathed her face. She opened her eyes. Then He rammed himself back into her body. She shook as he plunged back and forth, in and out.

He felt her body close over his penis. For the first time in his life he felt complete. He knew this is what he had wanted and was not surprised that Helen was his mate. His manhood wanted more and more of Helen. He never felt so relaxed and the world was wonderful. He found what he was looking so long and hard for ever. He had the body and wonder of Helen. It was her soul he sought and he made sure he found it!

"You are mine now, and forever." LaCount said to her

as he kissed her lips. "I shall be your husband. So it does not matter if I got you pregnant now. We shall marry in two weeks. One week we will be engaged, and the next married. I can't believe that you were a virgin. You waited for me to have you. I knew you were mine the second I saw you at the dock. Oh, my very own. I can not wait a week. We shall marry as soon as possible."

Her world was ended, anything she had hoped for now could never be. But then, it couldn't be when she was in England. Maybe she was just bad luck. She lay still next to the black skin of LaCount. She felt him touching her. What did it matter anymore? Brad her brother was dead, or he would have been here already, and her love, her love Edward, was just as dead.

He picked up her hand and kissed it. She pulled her hand away from his. He stared at her and laughed. "Put your hand back where I held it," he said.

His cold green eyes bored into her lake-blue eyes. She felt a chill run down her spine. She looked at her hand and slowly she placed it into his. He smiled at her.

"My dear," he said with a smile, "you are learning that you must do as I say and desire. You will find it much happier that way."

"Would you like to spend the night, or would you rather I take you back to your room. I would like you to spend the night here Helen. It would please me very much."

LaCount rubbed her velvet back. He had never known what it was to love as he did at that moment in time. His hand gently touched her golden hair and patted it back into it's place. He wanted her again. He just never wanted a woman like he wanted her right now.

He took her again. He knew her mind had slipped away from this loving. He could feel her breath on his face as he plunged into her again and again. He never thought he would love a white woman. Not only white, but a golden white woman, who answered his every dream. She was slim and white and gold, and god help him, she was a virgin when he entered her. He wasn't surprised but then, she had been to England.

He held her tightly to his chest, he was never going to let her go. No matter what happened, he was going to hold her fast and tight. He watched as she breathed against his chest. He pulled her even closer and closed his eyes. She would learn to love him, or at least fear him so much she would do as he wished with her.

He would have her again at twelve that night, and he would have her again in the morning. That is to say, if he could wait that long for his completeness. He was strong about most things, but he had never felt like he felt right this moment. He was a whole man, with a whole man's needs. His needs were Helen, and it did not matter what she felt now, she would learn her place. He needed her, but he would never tell her that. He knew he was on top of the world now and forever.

Chapter VII

MCGUIRE KNEW THE TRACKERS WERE near. He heard a scratch, it must be a match, and then he watched as a cheroot was lighted. They didn't care if he knew they were near or not. They were so sure of themselves. They were the best tractors on the Mississippi. LaCount would only use good killers and tractors. He would never use half measures. LaCount was New Orleans and New Orleans was a part of LaCount.

It was at that moment in time that McGuire knew he loved Clairese. He wanted her to know it to, but he thought she still loved LaCount. Why would anyone love that man? He was cruel and he thought only of himself. He never thought of anyone else. He was a one man show. He was all that counted.

McGuire wondered if he was doomed to always keep quiet about his love and who he loved. Was he always left holding the empty bag? First he thoughtlessly left his sister to her fate, and now he left Clairese to her fate. He watched the match flare in the night. He felt so helpless.

McGuire pulled Clairese close to his mouth. He whispered "No matter what happens stay right here in the crook of the tree."

Clairese turned her head and whispered back, "They will

see me in these white underclothing. What are you going to do?"

Pulling her even closer, his voice hoarse, "Your white under clothes are full of mud. They will never see you I'm going to leave you for a bit. No matter what, once again. Stay in this place. You understand. If you don't, you will get us both killed.".

Pushing back to the trunk of the tree, Clairese nodded in the dark. She had no hope left. She was doomed to die. What difference did it make. Here, later, whatever. The branch shook, as McGuire leaned into the next tree. Before she knew what was happening, McGuire was no longer next to her. She wanted to yell to him to come back, but it didn't matter. Her small hands gathered around her waist. She put her head against the tree trunk. She licked her dry lips. Tears dripped down her face. She tried to say a payer, but it stuck in her throat. Who was she to pray? She was the walking dead.

She held her breathing to a standstill. Clairese wondered if McGuire would ever know how she felt about him. She had the crazy notion that McGuire guessed she was still in love with LaCount. How would she ever tell him, that she loved him? Her heart beat in her breast. The goose bumps ran up and down her arms. She knew without anyone telling her, that McGuire would never believe that she loved him. He imagined her only love was LaCount, and that she was using him. Using him? She would trade her life for his. She wanted him to live, and so she would give her soul for that. If she had a soul to give after LaCount who had used her for his pleasure.

Clairese thought people in Church were fools. She wanted to be above any thing that made her one of the mob. She had to think like LaCount. Selfish! Nobodies fool! She was beautiful; she was like a picture, hanging for all to see, but none to touch as she was LaCount's woman.

Then it all changed. It was so subtle the change. She found out he loved someone else. It was the turning point in her life.

She depended on LaCount as her source of life. She wanted to have LaCount killed. She had hired, or she thought she had hired, someone who would kill him. What a laugh. They had told on her, on her! She could not believe that they told the men following her what she had tried to do. Why? Because LaCount was tired of her and she knew he was going to get a new mistress. She was finished; she was left over food for thought. What was it, two years, three, did it matter? How many years did he use her? Did it ever matter? He was tired of her and she was finished. She could hide, but not from LaCount. He would find her and he would kill her just as he had done to his other mistresses. He had no lose ends hanging around him. He was above the law. In fact, he was the law of New Orleans. He was powerful, rich and mean. He changed lovers as one changed their underwear. He grew tired of his present lover, then kill her and then find someone new and exciting. He wasted no time in the ritual.

"Please come back for me," whispered Clairese as she tried to pierce the darkness with her eyes. She thought of McGuire with her brain and knew they never would be together. Her life was full of sadness. Never had she had happiness. To have McGuire's love was something that would never happen, at least not to her.

All she could see was the dark shadows that spread out to the water. The water glowed in the darkness. It beckoned to her. Come join the fun it seems to say. It ended the road she traveled. She could smell the lighted cheroot and see its glow. Did they want her to know that they knew where she was?

McGuire quickly slipped from tree to tree. After slipping to ten trees, he climbed down to the ground. He knew those trackers were the best, but he had to find a way to kill them. All he had was the knife, his trusty knife. His knife had seen many a battle in the war, and after. He could trust this knife to save him. But how? It was a question of time and talent. It was a question of his having faith.

Slowly as the night started to get lighter, he could make out the shape of the two trappers. It was the half breed French/Indian, and the Big Man, the German hulk. What a pair. The Indian was the one to track and the German to kill. He crawled closer.

The Indian started to laugh as he looked at the tracks in the mud. "Ha, Ha, they think I can not tell they used the tracks to walk backwards. Ha. Ha."

A deep growl was issued out of the Big Man's mouth. He liked to kill with his bare hands. He hoped he would kill the girl slowly. First he would take her. Of course, if that little rat Indian wanted first - well, they could fight over that later. Truthfully, he was afraid of the Indian. He was fast and good with a knife. No, he would not fool around with that little half breed.

The Indian back tracked to the tree they climbed. "They went up there," he pointed. The Big Man just followed him. "See the mud? They probably jumped to another tree. Maybe they went inland. I think they are near."

The Big Man exhaled smoke from his cheroot. His little eyes examined the tree the Indian spoke of, but he saw nothing. The Indian had talent. He could see things others did not see. He also had a brain. He did not like the Big Man, but he put up with him as LaCount wanted him to do. The Big Man knew that the Indian hated his guts. He hated the fact that the Big Man killed without even a knife. He used his hands and squeezed and squeezed. The Big Man used his powerful hands to kill. He did not need a knife or gun. He was strong, but LaCount told him to follow the directions of the Indian, and he would follow. He did not want to end up as a log in the river. He did not want to end his life in a patch of grass that was faded. He followed whatever LaCount wanted. He might not have a brain, but he would do as he was told.

"Why are they close? They should be afraid of us," said the Big Man.

"They think they fooled us with the tree climb. But we know what they do," said the Indian. "They can not fool me."

"I sure would be miles from here," said the Big Man

"That is what they want us to think," said the Indian. "They will try something unexpected on us. We must watch our back."

The Indian climbed up the tree. He found traces of were they swung to another tree. He smiled. This was like taking candy from a baby. He was so sure of what they would do. An idea struck him. He climbed down the tree.

"Big Man, you go that way, and I will go this way. We will find them." Then he pulled the Big Man close to him. "They are near," he whispered. "Make believe you go that way, and I this. He will try to kill me, as I am little. You swing back and protect my back. Do You understand."

The Big Man nodded his head and started to walk to the left of the Indian. The Indian started to look up at the tree. He was sure that in a few seconds, or maybe minutes, McGuire would try to kill him. He walked slowly, to give McGuire a chance to come and get him.

The Big Man turned around and started slowly to follow the Indian. He walked softly on the grass for a man so big. He did not hear the footsteps that followed him. McGuire took his knife, and in one swift movement, jumped on the Big Man's large back. and plunged the knife into his neck. He Big Man tried to shrug him off, but the blood spurted out of his neck. He slowly sunk to the ground unable to make a sound. The Big Man tried to tell the Indian that he was knifed, but he held no breath to speak. He lay down on the ground and the mud sunk into his chest. His last memory was that the mud would swallow him whole. He was part of the landscape. Somehow, he never thought that he would die out in the wilderness. He thought he might die by LaCount, but never by himself left alone in place no one would look.

McGuire made sure he was dead, and took the Big Man's knife and pistol. Now he felt better about himself. A snap of a twig told him that someone was behind him. Turning around, McGuire saw it was the Indian; the Indian holding a pistol in his hands. The Indian laughed up a storm now that they faced each other.

"I wondered how to get rid of the pig of a German. Thanks. Now I get rid of you, then I get the girl and have her, then kill her. Everything worked as I planned."

"Don't think I haven't planned also," said McGuire as he smiled at the Indian.

"What you do? Wear iron vest? Ha, I have you cold," shouted the Indian

The Indian raised the pistol. McGuire knew his time had come. As a gambling man, he knew that life was cheap and he had played all his cards. He looked up and in amazement he saw Clairese. He was ready to jump and tell her it was too late. He saw something in her eyes. She was going to save him, even if it meant her death. Clairese jumped out of the tree on top of the Indian. They both fell down from her impact of the blow of the jump. Clairese rolled over and the Indian tried to get up. McGuire took his pistol and shot the Indian in the head. The Indian half up, fell down and did not move. Clairese smiled up at McGuire.

"Well, I ended up helping you after all," Clairese smiled "I saved your life like you saved mine. Now we are even." With a mighty chuckle, Clairese laughed and laughed. "Whoever thought the Indian had a sixth sense? He didn't even know I was above him. He was too cocky, believing he had won."

"I can't believe you saved my life. You are something else," chuckled McGuire.

"Hey, what are friends for?" asked Clairese

"Friends are for saving a fellows life, I think," laughed McGuire.

McGuire helped her up and checked out if she had any

broken bones. Turning around and around, Clairese proved she was all in one piece. She posed and primped as she turned one way and then another. She smiled happily. She sang, "I am the best."

"You are the best," said McGuire. "Clairese, would you believe that I have feelings for you-"

"Please, don't say anything else," Clairese turned away from him. She did not want him to see the hope in her eyes.

He turned her around and held her by her shoulders. "Clairese-"

"You feel something for me, because I saved your life. There is nothing else to say about it. I understand." Clairese looked him in the eyes as she stated this fact. She wanted it to be different, bit she understood. She was just a girl and she saved his life. He a Southerner could never love a half black woman. He was brought up differently than she was, and there was no hope or love lost over the South and what they felt about blacks.

McGuire looked at her and shook his head. He had bigger things to think about. His mind was in a whirl as he wanted to impress on Clairese that he did love her, but he had to think of his sister also. He was lost in his mind.

"We got to find a faster way to get to New Orleans. Helen is in trouble. I can feel it. We have to find a boat and ride the river. Where I don't know, but we have to. There is no way we can go into any town and rent a carriage or a horse. Look at you. No clothing, just your underpants and top. Look at me, no gun, well, now I have one, and I look like a pirate. We are muddy, and our clothing looks like it was shot into the river and wrung out."

Clairese stared at McGuire. "I don't think there are any boats to be had. I do not think we can go into town. They would stone me as a whore. Of course, that is what I really am. Well, not really, I was LaCount's mistress. Guess that makes me a whore, hey? But a special one."

McGuire stared at her. No, there was no way they could go into any town. People would really stare at them like crazy. There was something nagging on his brain. No way had those two trappers walked all the way here. They must have horses somewhere tied up. He had to find those horses. He would back track. Yes, that was it. They had come on horseback, and there must be about three horses. One for each, and then one for supplies.

McGuire stared at the long way down the Mississippi River. The trackers had to hide their horses somewhere. They had to tie them someplace easy for them to find. They had to tie them to something. A tree, a branch, something, they tied them to something and it had to be close. They would not want to be without transportation with their prisoners. The Big Man and the Indian were so sure that they would find Clairese and McGuire. They were caught too easily. Was that part of their plan? He must think and think like them. But, they never would think of their being dead LaCount would not want them alive. They had to be dead and carried back. They needed horses.

"We have to find their horses," said McGuire to Clairese.

Clairese looked at McGuire with longing. She would never have him love her. She wanted him so badly. Would he at least take her for a mistress? She would be willing to at least be near him that way. It all seemed so useless. She nodded her head to McGuire.

"I guess we better look for the horses. We can be in New Orleans shorter than walking in this mud. I am so sick of mud and snakes." Clairese mumbled.

McGuire looked at Clairese. He wanted to assure her of his love for her, but he knew she would not believe it now. Her idea of solid Southern men came from LaCount and what he taught her about what a Southern man deemed proper. Didn't she realize he was no longer a Southern man?

McGuire motioned for Clairese to follow him. He watched

were he stepped. He was following their trail. Never had he thought that he would follow the trackers tracks. He walked slowly. He was not as expert as the trackers, but he was pretty good, well, fair. He hungered down at the ground. His eyes traveled over the ground that was near him. He noticed a pebble was turned, from the dirt that was now facing up instead of down.

"I think we are on their trail, Clairese. At least I hope we are," said McGuire.

Clairese drew in her breath. She surely hoped they would find horses. "We can be out of here and away before the other half looks for us."

"The other half?" questioned McGuire

"Never mind. Let's just find the horses and be on our way. I can't tell you how I wish I died in the water. It sure is better than having all that snake, and turtle." Clairese whispered.

Eyeing the land, he stepped forward again. He saw a bush that had broken a stem near the ground. Good, he was nearer the Big Man's and Indian's horses; he could feel the horses near. The Big Man and the Indian would never walk far. They could follow tracks, but there were none until now. So he moved slowly forward. Then he heard a soft snicker. The horse, the horse, he wanted to cry. I found the horses. A first he stood still. Then his heart began to pound. He knew he had found the horses.

"Clairese, I think we have found the horses. We can ride to New Orleans now. I have to look and make sure that there are horses," cried McGuire.

Running wildly, McGuire went to the sound he heard. Around the bend of the land he saw the horses tied to a tree. He had found the horses. They had a way to get to New Orleans. After that, well, the way they were dressed was another story. But now, they were going to New Orleans, and they should make it pretty quickly. He could not believe his good luck.

"Come on Clairese, we have Horses," he cried.

Clairese came running up to where he stood. She looked at the horses as if they were coated with gold. "They are horses." she cried.

McGuire took her by the waist and swung her around and around. "We're on our way. We can travel quickly. Look they even have food. We can eat first, and then be on our way. We can strip those men, and you can put on the small Indian's clothing. We can make you look like a man, that is until we can find a way to make you back to a woman. We have weapons, we have food, and we have clothing. My God, we are lucky that they came our way. I was in despair."

"I wonder why they were so sure that they could capture us?" Clairese said as she looked at all the food to be eaten. There was cans and cans of food.

Clairese started to cry as she took the food out of the pack the horses were carrying. She found a can opener. She opened up a can of beans and just dipped her fingers in and gulped down the food. She opened another can and crammed peaches into her mouth. McGuire took a can and opened it. He had beans and he ate with his fingers.

"I never realized how much I love food," McGuire said as he stuffed more food into his mouth.

Clairese sat down on the muddy ground. "The Indian's clothing will fit me fine. I can clean up and slip into his clothing. I will look like a wild Indian with my wild hair and big breasts."

"Wear a poncho over your top half," McGuire said as he stripped the horses down and rubbed them down. "The horses need some care, if we are going to ride them hard to get to New Orleans by the end of tomorrow."

Clairese went to the river and started to wash up with her chemise. She took it off her breast and washed it in the river. Then she used it to wash her top, and feet. She went back to the Indian and stripped him. She pulled off her pantaloons and pulled on his leather pants. They fit her snuggly. She pulled on his shirt and went back to the horses. She found a poncho on the ground were McGuire had thrown everything so he could rub the horse down.

"I'm all clean. I fit into the Indians clothing. I look like a wild Indian to be sure, but then so what?" asked Clairese.

"You look like a princess. You are a beautiful girl. I want you to believe me when I say you are so pretty. When will you believe me?" asked McGuire.

"The day the moon turns to blue." answered Clairese. "But I thank you for saying it to me. I need some assurance that I am alive."

She washed her hair in the river and pulled it back into a pony tail. She looked at McGuire as he rubbed the horses down. She watched his muscles ripple as he worked. His hair shone in the bright sun light. Gold! Gold she thought. Never be mine, but oh, how I love it. She was falling in love with a man that did not know she was alive. A man who would never look at her with love, but she didn't care. She wanted him and she would have him, one way or the other.

"Feels good to be clean. I most miss the baths I use to take," said Clairese as she smiled at the sun.

"I'm going to clean up. I too miss the baths I took. Guess we will do fine once we get to New Orleans and straighten it all out." replied McGuire.

"Will we ever straighten it all out?" asked Clairese

"All we can do is try," replied McGuire.

The horses shone in the sunlight. One was a big black, the other was a brown smaller horse, but he looked like he could outrun anything. The pack horse was just a plodding horse as far as Clairese could see.

McGuire went to the river and washed himself down. He took off all his clothing and washed his lean long body. He felt good. He washed his hair. His hair sparkled in the light. He gleamed in the light.

McGuire went to the big man, and pulled off all his

clothing. McGuire made a face at the rubbish that lay on the clothing. "Not the cleanest person alive, I do declare. How did he stand himself? He must have smelled how awful his armors were to everyone near him."

McGuire pulled on the Big Man's pants, shirt, and his gun belt. The gun belt was too big around for McGuire to wear. He shrugged it over his shoulder. He pulled one of the ropes that the horses had been used to tie them to tie his pants.

"That Big Man was really big. Look at these pants. If it weren't for the rope used to tie the horses with I could not even hope to wear the pants." grumbled McGuire.

"You look like a balloon," laughed Clairese

"Well, at least I can wear them now. I see you stuffed yourself with the food. So it is time we got going," said McGuire as he used his hands to comb his hair into place. His hair still fell over one eye. He looked like a pirate, with those big baggy pants, the guns over his shoulder, and his half smile.

"Clairese, we have to hurry. I'm sure that LaCount also called in the Odge brothers. I bet they're on the other side of the river. I'm sure they have a way of telling each other what they find. They have to have some sort of code, or maybe fire, or-well, who knows. I know we got to get out of here as quickly as we can. Those are not boys we want to tangle with. The Odge brothers will be like hornets finding out that we killed the Indian and the Big Man. I hate to see what they will do once they get riled up, to say the least. . Well, I'm betting, and I am a betting man. They have to be coming our way, and soon. We got to get moving."

"I hate to tell you, I don't know how to ride a horse." Clairese said as she trembled at the huge horses.

"You don't know how to ride?" asked McGuire.

"Leave me, go to your sister. I can take care of myself."

"Never! We are a team. And a team stays together." shouted McGuire

"A team? I have never been part of a team. Are you sure? I

will slow you down an awful lot. I don't know the first thing about riding a horse." Clairese shook her head.

McGuire smiled at her. "We will leave the pack horse behind and I will swing you up on the horse. You just hold on. Can you do that Clairese?"

"I will hold on." whispered Clairese.

"Good girl." said McGuire.

Clairese shook her head and cleared her mouth from the water she was drinking. She looked up at McGuire and all she could think about, was she wanted him. No matter what happens, she wanted him and she wanted him so badly. Her body shook when ever she looked at him. He swung up on the back of the horse. Clairese trembled at the height of the horse. She looked around and saw the dead men where they lay so naked. They looked odd so naked without any clothing. Flesh laying still, that once was a living man. Clairese breathed through her mouth and shook her head. It could be her that lay so still. A thought flashed across her mind and she felt a tear run down her face. She was so lucky that McGuire tried to save her, but was all lost? She did not move on the horse and the horse stood still. McGuire watched her as she sat on the horse.

"Pick up the reins and shake them a little. The horse will go," stated McGuire.

Clairese with trembling heart shook the reins. Her heart stood still as the horse moved. She felt herself sliding off the horse. It was a long way down.

Clairese landed in the mud. McGuire just shook his head and got off the horse and picked her up.

"I guess it will be awhile before you can ride. We will take it easy. How about you ride up with me and we let the horse follow by my holding the reins?"

Clairese smiled. "I would love that."

McGuire picked her up and put her on the saddle on the big black horse. He jumped up and held her tenderly around her waist. Clairese regarded McGuire and his hard muscles of his hand that wrapped around her body. Heaven the touch of McGuire. So Clairese rode with McGuire double on the one horse. McGuire clutches the ends of the brown horse in his hand. The horse followed along without any trouble.

McGuire was right, thought Clairese, there must be some signal that told each man where and what they saw and what they were doing. They had a hard ride ahead of them. Yet, Clairese could only think of one thing. She wanted McGuire and she would have him. How or why she did not know but she was sure that she would have him. Even if he refused her, she would have him.

"We're not making time riding double. Maybe I should just stay behind," Clairese said as she clutched the shirt of McGuire.

"I already told you, we are a team and we stay together," said McGuire

"But it is so slow to go this way. I didn't think it would be so slow," answered Clairese.

Clairese felt her stomach churn as she looked at McGuire. He was so handsome and strong. Would he want a half breed like her? She wanted so desperately for him to like her. His smile was worth all the money that Clairese ever made or had. She preened herself in her Indian Outfit. She felt the soft hide of the animal. She wondered what animal had sacrificed itself for this Indian outfit. But then her eyes looked at McGuire. She smiled as she looked at him. She sat so close to him she could feel his heart.

He noticed her smile. He smiled back. He lifted his hand in a salute to her and for her help. "Well girl, I guess we better ride for leather. No telling what the other people are doing now. Probably looking to kill us. So let's get ourselves on the road."

"I'm ready to go wherever you say. Do whatever you want, and McGuire, we will make it to New Orleans to save your sister. I swear I will not hold you up," whispered Clairese as her mouth moved nearer to McGuire's mouth.

McGuire looked at her mouth, and he knew the world was turned upside down. His manhood became strong and he wanted to kiss Clairese here and now. He held himself back with a strong lecture about his sister.

As the horse lopped along, Clairese moved to McGuire's face. She held her breath as she leaned into his body.

"I want you McGuire, what do you say to that?" whispered Clairese

"I want you also. I want you so much, Clairese, I can not tell you how hard it is for me to love you, when you still love LaCount." whispered McGuire,

"I do not love LaCount. I love you. Can you understand that? Can you live with it? I have wanted you when you saved me in the Mississippi River. That is how long I have wanted you." Clairese drew closer to McGuire.

"You say that Clairese, but do you mean it? Do you really mean it?" asked McGuire.

Their lips touched. McGuire put his other hand around Clarisse's waist. The reins of the horse dropped from McGuire's hand. His lips turned hard as rock as he kissed Clairese. Clairese moved her lips closer to his and holding her became a matter of life or death.

"Oh, Clairese, I have dreamed of you in my arms," the yearning voice came from McGuire.

Clairese closed her eyes. Their bodies blended into one. Energy, turned into a slippery saddle. They both fell to the ground, but they did not notice. McGuire held Clairese so close they were like one. McGuire's hands felt the breast of Clairese. His hands roamed down to untie the Indians pants.

"Clairese, do you mean what you say? Have you forgotten your love of LaCount? I want you now. Can you understand that?" whispered McGuire.

"Love, take me now. I have wanted you forever. Can't you

see that. I love you. I am willing to be anything you want. I must have you now." Clairese said as her arms went into his open shirt. Her hands caressed the blond hair on his chest.

For the first time in the year, McGuire sensed he was whole. He would try to stop, but he could not. He had to have Clairese now, just as sure as the world turned on its axis. He had to feel whole and new right new. He grabbed her pants and tore them from her body. Clairese trembled with the fire that consumed her. They lit together like dynamite. There was no holding them back. They became one and the world stopped and the mud became a bed of feathers.

Time stood still as McGuire plunged into Clairese. She moaned and groaned in her throat as if she could not live another moment without McGuire's love. He entered heaven as he took Clairese back and forth, in and out. He was once again a man. He was no longer a looker in, but a participant of the world. He was in love with this woman, who now held his heart in her hands.

"Clairese, I love you. I do so love you," roared McGuire.

"I want you so. I want to be with you forever," replied Clairese. "Can you understand that? Can you be mine forever and a day?"

Their arms held tightly against each body. They paused for a second. Their breathing came harshly out. Then they looked into each other's eyes. Lake-blue eyes clashed with the gray-black eyes. And then, the eyes seemed to smile at each other. It was with love that they gazed at each other. It was total and complete love that they stared at each other. It was plain that they would love forever.

Once their eyes met with laughter. "We're more dirty now than before our bath," laughed Clairese

"No dirtier than the Big Man's clothing were. Only more muddy." laughed McGuire.

"How will I clean the Indian's clothing. He was so meticulous about his clothing?" asked Clairese

"You'll have to sponge it. No other way."

"I guess I just jump into the river to clean up. I'll help you clean the Indian's clothing."

"I would never expect this waste of time for you," declared Clairese. "I'll be as quick as can be cleaning his clothing. I hate for you to waste your time being with me. I truly think you go on without me. It will be for the best."

"Clairese, I can never leave you. Especially, after what we did together. I love you. You make me whole. We will start anew in Texas. I will raise horses. I know all about that. We raised horses on the plantation. We can do it out West. I don't have to be a gambling man, I can be a horse man and trainer."

Chapter VIII

THE CABIN THEY GAVE TO Helen was no more than a closet. It held a small bed, her small trunk, and a bowl on the floor for her to wash. It was like a box without a porthole at least to give a semblance of balance.

She knew that traveling without a companion left her vulnerable. It was the reason she had to hole up in the ship during the day. It was a matter of principal that McLeon even gave her a place to live. She realized it was a favor to her brother, that she was even on board. But McLeon looked at her so strangely. What was he thinking every time he saw her? She could not think of why, but she had known him all her life, so it must be he was worried about her being alone on the ship.

"Abe, the cabin is a box of nothing but a bed and my trunk," cried Helen. "Can't you give me something bigger?"

"Helen, I would if I could. But this is a ship that carries cargo, not passengers. I thought you realized that when we snuck you aboard."

"Yes, I did. But I never thought I'd be boxed up in a little tiny room. It is no bigger than a pencil. Abe, I can't sit there all day without anything to do." said Helen.

"Look, I promised Brad I would bring you to your aunt.

I will keep that promise. But Helen, you have to cooperate in part. I can not make the ship bigger."

"I know that. It's so terrible to sit there and have nothing to do. I have very little clothing. I have no books to read. I just sit there and think of all the terrible things that might happen on this trip."

"Nothing is going to happen on this trip. Just be patient. I can not help you in any respect. I have a ship to run, a crew that is trying to see you and what you do and who you are. I have my hands full." said Abe.

Helen looked at Abe with sorrowful eyes. She was so use to getting her own way in everything she did. She was a flirt, and she knew it. Should she flirt with Abe to get her way, or be satisfied that he even let her on board? Helen decided she better be good, or he might throw her overboard.

Helen felt the rise and fall of the water. She was so tired of being on this ship. It had taken days for her to stop her stomach from churning with the sea. But she was never sea sick. Thank Heavens for that. That was the reason for the big bowl on the floor or her cabin. For sea sick!

Yet, she could hardly wait to feel solid land beneath her feet. If it wasn't for Brad, her brother, she would not be on this ship. He knew Abe McLeon and was best friends with him. He had Abe promise to deliver her to her aunt. As a Southern gentleman, he had to keep his promise. Brad had found enough money to pay Abe to take her. At least enough for her food. He never did find enough to pay for her passage on a real ship. He insisted she go because she had no hope left in the states. She was going to go back to her mother's roots. England! London! Home?

The terrible war between the states was over, and there was nothing left of their plantation. There was no money now, and no hope for it to get better. Their mother and father were dead. Killed by union men. What could she expect of the union? Killed over a skinny chicken. So much loss. Nothing left.

There was no bringing back the life they had. It was a no win situation. Brad her brother was at loose ends and he did not find peace with himself, or with life. He didn't know what to do after fighting for the South. He was lucky that the Union did not know of his fighting for the South. They would not let him roam free as he did. They, the union, wanted blood.

Helene knew they would land today in England. She could see the land of the Thames and the houses and the castles. She caught her breathe as she felt the air around her suddenly feel warm and welcome. She was a person without a home or heritage. She felt so alone. Would they welcome her? Would they take her in? What was her fate to be?

Her dearly sainted mother had come from London. Her mother always wanted Helen to visit London, but to come back to the Plantation to live. No other life was as good or as wonderful as Plantation life. Though her mother was English to her very roots, Mrs. McGuire had loved the South and all it stood for- Pride, richness, society, passion, and a world of their own. She would never give up her pride in the plantation. She would never leave her home for anything that was of the old school. She, Helen's mother loved the life she lived and thought it would go on forever. It was such a shock that the North hated the South and all it stood for.

Helen had gone across the ocean in the care of Captain Abe McLeon, a close friend of the McGuire's during the plantation days. Captain McLeon was the youngest son of the plantation next to the McGuire's. Brad and Abe went to the same school together, in fact, they were roommates. They could not be closer. He was also the best friend of Brad McGuire during the war. That was why Brad asked Captain McLeon to watch over her.

McLeon demanded that Helen stay in her cabin at certain times of the day. That Helen could only walk outside when the sun was about to set. Some days, he would not let her out of his sight. He was a tyrant. He had promised Brad McGuire that he would be sure to see Helen was put into the capable hands of Lady Grace Hope, sister of Helen's mother. He would see his duty and he would do it, come whatever Helen thought.

"I have to get out of that cabin. All I do is count nails in the wall. Please, let me out." cried Helen

"As long as I have to watch over you, you stay in that cabin. It's bad enough the cabin boy serves you three meals a day. At first they thought it was a Yankee or some man, on the run, but that cabin boy has a big mouth. He tells all the sailors it is a woman. He says how pretty you are. I can not stop him, but I sure would like to shot him. I can't whip all of sailors. So stay hidden and be good."

"Why whip them?" asked Helen

"You know good and well. I can't let them near you. What is wrong with you to even want that? You are so pretty even I want you. How about that?" asked Abe. "Do you know how hard it is for me. Think of the crew. Oh, they know your there, but that is it. Right now they only think of you. What if they saw you. We would have a revolt. You know it is true. So be good a stay in your cabin until I let you have some air."

Helen faced the captain. "Do you really think I'm Pretty?"

"Damn right I do. If you weren't Brad's sister I would have my way with you, and you know that." said Abe as he turned his bright eyes on Helen. "I have loved you since you were 14. Do you think I am made of iron?"

"You loved me? Do you still?" asked Helen in amazement.

"I have loved you so long and hard. What was I to do? You're rich and spoiled. Me a second son. I got me a boat. I was going to make it work. Then the war came. You were lost to me. I knew you would never love me like I loved you."

"But you were Brad's friend. You always hated it when I followed after you boys." said Helen as she looked down at her skirt.

"No, I pretended to hate it. I loved you for so long. I still do. Run away with me. I love you Helen. I really and truly do."

"Oh Abe, I have to go to my mother's sister now. It is too late. I have to tell you truly, I do not love you and never have."

Abe looked at her with all the love he had in his heart. He stood very still.

Helen turned a bright pink and then turned back to her cabin. She never thought of Abe wanting her. It was an unheard of situation as far as she was concerned. Abe, the steadiest man of them all. Captain of his own ship. Abe, she thought, as she stumbled back to her cabin. She liked Abe McLeon, but she did not love him and knew she never would. Run away with him. It sounded so delicious. So delightful! So thrilling! Her mind thought about it for a second, and then she discarded it. It was just a dream.

Helen's mother was Linda. She was the second sister to be born, and Grace Hope was the eldest sister. Linda wanted the world on a silver platter. She could not be controlled. To say that Linda was a handful, would be putting it mildly. Linda was wild, and she could not be contained in the stiff English society she was brought up in. Though raised from a child at the idea of being from rich peers, she was always different and intense in her desire to be herself. She defied convention. She wanted something different, something unheard of, something rare.

Linda wore a white dress that swirled and whirled, The dress made from chiffon and lace, hugged her waist with small embroidered roses running the length of her waist. She understood that she was stunning in the dress, and when she smiled, she was divesting. As she danced, the noticed Brad McGuire. Linda had never seen a man who was handsomer than he was. She had to meet Brad McGuire at this party she was attending. Linda decided then and there she would marry him, and only him.. He was at a party that Lord George gave for his sister. Brad stood out. He was so tall, he towered over everyone. As soon as she saw him, she fell madly in love with him. She imitated him. Linda spoke like he did, slow and easy. Even his walk was slow and easy. He was in no rush to go anywhere. But he did notice Linda. She made sure he noticed her, when she smiled. She smiled at him and he could not take his eyes off her.

Linda's dress encased her as she stood before Brad McGuire. She looked into his lake-blue eyes. She was enchanted by his build and his manner. She drew in a breath. Linda sidled up to him and smiled. It was the smile that smote him at once. He too fell madly in love with Linda. He had never been one to like the ladies, and here he was staring at her face as if it was the last thing he ever would see.

"I'll only be here a few days." Brad Sr. said as he took her hand into his large hand.

Linda looked up at his sky blue eyes and shook her head. "My, but you are tall. I bet you are taller than any one here."

"I bet you're the sweetest girl there is here." said Brad Sr.

"No, not sweet, but here I am." said Linda as she squeezed his hand. They had eyes for only themselves. It was strange to see, as Linda never looked at anyone like she looked at Brad, Sr.

"Have you ever been to the New World?" asked Brad.

"No, but it is something I would adore seeing. I like new things. I like to make my own mind up on what it sees and hears." replied Linda as a blush covered her face.

By mutual consent, they spent the rest of the night together while the party lasted. They ate together, they danced together, and they smiled at each other looking into each others eyes.

Brad, Sr. held her close. "Will you go with me to the plantation? Will you marry me? I know we only met tonight, but I feel like I can not bare to lose you ever. "

"Yes," said Linda. "I would follow you to the ends of the earth."

"I believe I am in love with you," said Brad Sr. "I never felt this way about any lady. You are special. I love everything about you."

"I know I'm in love with you," said Linda and she smiled and smiled. It was a wide and welcome smile.

Linda ran off and married Brad, Sr. on the ship that was taking him back to the New World. She never told her parents, or her sister. She just left and went with her new husband Brad, Sr. She was madly in love with him and nothing any one said worried her. She was gone with Brad, Sr. across the ocean to his land. She never worried that her parents worried about her. She just didn't care or think. She was wild with happiness. When she was settled, she wrote her parents about her marriage. She was not ashamed that she loved Brad, Sr. She was insane with happiness. There they lived happily their dream of happily ever after. Linda gave birth to two children, Brad and Helen. Linda and Brad, Sr were happy and content with their life.

Grace, the eldest sister of Linda's , married a peer named Milton Hope. She never was blest with children. She had dreamed of having a daughter to look after to dress and present to court. She wanted to buy clothing and have invitations to all the Ton's parties. She dreamed of the fun she was missing. She was a hopeless romantic and thought of the fun she would have with a daughter. She wanted a daughter so desperately. When she got the letter that Helen would live with her, her dreams of what would be came true. She was in ecstasy.

Helen stood for a second on deck as the ship made its way down the Thames to London. She noted the crowds and the noise. She watched as the ship anchored in the harbor at the many different buildings that seemed to grow from the ground up. There were so many different people in different dress. Sailors from the Navy, and beggars and fashionably dressed men and women. The world on the wharf teamed with the hustle and bustle, of men and women. Helen's eyes grew wide as she studied the scene. It was so different than what she knew.

Her life had been so tame compared to this scene. Here was life with a capital L.

The crew of the ship Helen sailed on, saw her for the first time. They lapsed in wonder that this beautiful lady had traveled by herself to England. They suddenly realized that their Captain, Abe McLeon hid her from the crew. They understood for the first time, what a terrible burden their captain had been under. No wonder he acted like he had crawling ants all over his body. Not only did he have the responsibility of seeing her to England he was in love with the lady passenger. They could see how he watched her with longing. No way the Captain would have the lady, she was gone with the look in her eyes-expectation.

The wind blew the golden curls of Helen's hair, and her oval face looked up into the sky. Her thin reed like body was 5 feet 3 inches. She came from a family of giants, and she was the dwarf. He father was well over six feet seven inches tall, and her mother was taller than Helen. But the war had broken her family. Her mother and father had been killed over a chicken. It all seemed so senseless now. The Yankees wanted the chicken; her mother tried to hide the chicken; and her father protected the hole the chicken was living in. The Yankee found the hole with the chicken and shot them, her mother and father, for hiding the chicken. The chicken was only skin and bones. It didn't matter to the Yanks, the soldier shot her mother and father over food that was not even eatable.

There was nothing left of their plantation. Brad had gone off to war and came back a man without a path to follow. She had been hidden half the war and the other half she had been put up with Mrs. Carp, a Northern Lady. It was Abe McLeon who had asked Mrs. Carp for help in hiding Helen. McLeon even though he was Southern, he still knew many Northern people. Mrs. Carp was a rich lady, who was also a widow. McLeon knew her before the war as he was a captain of his own vessel. He supplied Mrs. Carp with various sundries.

McLeon lost his ship during the war, so he sought out Brad his best friend and they spent the war together. Mrs. Carp was a kind lady, who worried about the people who were fighting in the war.

Mrs. Carp had said she would help Helen and she did. She made Helen her maid. Helen only had to serve when people visited. Other than that, Helen was free to stay in her room. No one would doubt Mrs. Carp's word as she was rich. Mrs. Carp knew Helen was a Southerner, from Helen's speech. She surely knew she was from the South. So she told Helen not to talk when anyone visited her. Just to serve whatever and leave. She put Helen in a gray dress that hung on her slim frame. Few people even noticed Helen and her drab dress. She was just a maid. Helen lived with Mrs. Carp, but she was so lonely. She stayed in her room most of the time. There was little else to do. Mrs. Carp gave Helen books to read. Time did not drag, because of the books that covered all subjects from stars to romance.

After the war, Brad won enough money that he could send her to England where there was family. He had enough money for the food that Helen would eat, and not enough for a regular ticket on a regular ship. He had to send her to England, and the only ship he had enough money for that, was on the ship that Captain McLeon was captain McLeon had his ship back and he was going to go across the ocean to England. He was Brad's friend from when they went to university together, and then the war between the states. Helen thought what a friend he was to her. He made her stay in her cabin almost the whole trip, so that it would not disrupt his crew. Helen was happy to at last leave her cabin as the ship made its way to London. Her pink rose bud mouth stretched into a broad smile. England., seemed so wonderful as she would be free to be herself again. England did not have the burnt out buildings that covered the south. Here the buildings stood proud and tall. She felt clean for the first time in years. A new beginning was opening for her.

Helen was wracked with sorrow that Abe McLeon loved her. She could never love him, she thought of him as her brother's friend. Nothing more! The ship docked and sailors rushed here and there with ropes and pulling chains. The gangway lowered with a soft bang. Abe followed Helen down the gang plank. He was sorry to see her go. He was in love with Helen, who never looked at him with any type of love. Helen came down the gang plank in her light green traveling dress, with hooped skirt hit the rail as she walked. She wore her little perched hat with feathers and her light green gloves and her little receptacle. Her jacket fit her slim body like a second skin, and the blouse underneath the jacket was a pure white, that shone in the sun. Helen looked like a very pretty doll.

Lady Grace Hope watched as Helen came down the gang plank. She noted Abe following her like a man in love. She saw Helen, and knew this was her niece. She looked exactly like the rest of the family, slim with golden hair. Lady Grace Hope stood very still as she watched Helen descend the gang plank. Lady Grace thought Helen was as graceful as any ballerina. Finally, Helen looked at Lady Grace. Helen knew immediately, this was her aunt. She looked just like her mother even the same height.

Picking up her skirts, Helen ran to Lady Grace. Putting up her hand, Lady Grace stopped Helen from hugging her. "My, my, you are a fine girl. Your mother loved that old plantation. Never could understand that. Told her she should have married here in England. Like I did. A much more sane nation than your crazy warring nation. Ladies do not hug in public my dear. You must learn to act like one now that you have come to live here"

Helen dropped her hands and stared at Lady Grace. "Sorry, I guess my plantation days are showing."

"It is all right now. I want you to act and be the best. From now on, you just follow what I say. I am so glad to have you here. I bet you broke every heart around." said Lady Grace as she smiled into Helen's eyes. "You are as pretty as your mother was."

"My mother looked just like you do," said Helen

Lady Grace smiled. She wondered if the child understood that she looked so long to have a daughter. Now, she had her wish. Lady Grace did not say a word.

Lady Grace lifted a finger and her footman appeared. She pointed to Helen's luggage and she led Helen to her coach. "You know hooped skirts are quite out, my dear. We shall have to get you a complete wardrobe before I present you to the ton and the Royalty. My, my, that should be fun. I haven't had a child to love, you know. So this will give me something I longed to do. Dress a daughter and present her to the Royals."

Looking at the complete picture of Lady Grace, Helen saw she wore a bustle in the back of her dress and not the large hoop she was wearing. Lady Grace was tall and slim and she looked just like her mother. Lady Grace had silver hair, and eyes of light blue, not the Lake-blue eyes that Brad and she had. Their eyes made their faces stand out in a crowd. They took after their father with their eyes.

Lady Grace was dressed all in purple. Her hat, suit, gloves, shoes, blouse, and receptacle surrounded Lady Grace like a grape skin. Lady Grace had a big smile. She was so happy that at last she could go to the balls the ton held. She felt that she was in her glory.

"We are going to have so much fun," Lady Grace said as she pleated her skirt with her hands.

"I don't want you to worry too much about me. I can take anything you want me to do." Helen gasped as she looked at the velvet seats of the coach.

The coachman helped the two ladies inside the coach. The coach started and the two ladies tried to understand each other. "You look just like your mother," said Lady Grace. "Same grace, and same oval face. You do have your father's eyes. Lake-blue. They are so startling in your face with your golden hair. Of course, your mother was so much taller than you. Can't imagine were you came from. "

Helen smiled at Lady Grace. "It is so good of you to take me in. I can not tell you all the terrible things that happened to our plantation. It is just a burnt out ruin. But the marble columns are charred but still standing. seems so lost. Brad, my brother, I worry about him. I think between the war and the lost plantation, Brad is rootless for a time. I hope he finds himself."

"Let's get you settled with some nice young man. I shall give you a coming out party. It will be the best treat I can think of for myself. I always wanted a daughter so I could have a great party. My goodness. So much to do. We will worry about Brad at a later date. Let us enjoy this time together."

"A party for me?" asked Helen. "It is so nice, I can not believe it. I haven't been to a party in so long. We use to have one all the time. It was the way of life. A life that is gone forever. My mother loved giving parties. She loved living in the South."

Lady Grace just smiled "I think it will be a small party. That way I can see what you need to learn. Manners, that is. Especially, you being an American. It will be hard a first, but we shall overcome. "

Helen sat very still. She watched Lady Grace as she stared out the window. Helen knew she should do as Lady Grace did. So Helen stared out the window of the coach.

They rode for over an hour over a road that was well graded. Finally when they turned into a road that curved and curved it was not as well graded as the road they had left. The trees seemed to drape over the road like a cloak. The day became darker and darker but still a small amount of light filtered through the trees. In the dull light, there in front of them was a large red brick house. It was square but big, with a white trim around the windows and the doorways.

Helen gasped. The house was so large, so square, so

uninviting. It looked more like a prison or hospital then a house. "This is my husband's ancestral home. Disgusting isn't it? Well one does learn to live in it after awhile. Not much chance of changing it my dear. Solid. That is all I can say for it. But the inside, oh, I have fixed the inside. There is the loveliest furniture. Delicate and carved. The drapes are of satin and some are of velvet. The sofas are covered in various shades of blue. Yes. It will do you justice. You should always wear blue. It has been so long since we had a party. I can just about believe in fairy tales."

"Of course, we will have a party to introduce you to some of the people who live around here. Then we shall have a ball for your coming out party in London. I just love London. It is so--how do you say, perfect." bubbled Aunt Grace. "Of course we have to have you dressed better than you are. My, you look so old hat to say the least. But we shall fix that. I have called my seamstress already. She should be at the house now. I just knew you would not have the right clothing."

Helen just stared at her aunt. She was so bubbly and outgoing. Aunt Grace did not know what it was to have a burnt out home and no place to go. Thankfully, she Helen, did have a place to go, but Brad. Poor Brad, what will he do?

Inside the brick house rooms seemed to flow and grow at an angle. It was the chapel that greeted Helen. The chapel was a room that they entered through the inside garden. It seemed to grow as it was bathed with the flowers and long white candles that came from the inside garden. The chapel was small and had few seats. There on the walls hung the tapestries of long ago. Even though it was old the chapel had a fresh smell of flowers and wax. This was the first place Lady Grace took Helen.

"We worship here every Sunday. Though sometimes, we go to the big church. I think we will go to the big church so people will see you. Yes, it is a good idea to go this Sunday. I hope you have some dresses by then. I don't want to wait too long to introduce you to the gentry." said Lady Grace as she looked over at Helen.

The days flew by, with dressmakers, and shoe makers, receptacles, and parasols, and under clothing, and hair cutting. Helen did not have time to think Then came the day of the party just for the neighbors. It was a lovely evening with the stars shinning brightly in the night.

This was the first that Aunt Grace was giving to see how Helen reacted to the people, but most of all, how the Ton reacted to her. Aunt Grace did not have to worry. Helen had been brought up to be a Lady, and even if she spoke funny, she had the grace and knowledge of how to act, eat and speak.

The house was decorated with items of purple and blue. The decorations shined in the light of the candles. There were hundreds of candles framing the big ball room. Drapes covered the walls and windows. Aunt Grace realized she had missed these party decorations and the parties because she had no daughter. She was so proud that Helen had come. Now she was part of the Ton.

As the neighbors arrived, Helen noticed the very tall man entering the house. His eyes she noted were a stormy gray and his hair was so blond, it looked almost white. His face was stern, he had a Roman nose, and a very square chin. His lips were full, and as he looked at her, his lips took on a funny crooked smile. Their eyes met. Helen felt like she had never been devoured so intently by those eyes that held her motionless.

Aunt Grace and Uncle Milton were busy greeting all their guests and introducing them to Helen. It seemed like hundreds of people coming for this "small" party of neighbors that Aunt Grace was throwing. Helen could not imagine what a large party was for Aunt Grace.

Uncle Milton was a mild man., small, five feet six inches tall, with brown hair and eyes. He seemed to take whatever Aunt Grace did in his stride. He smiled with a little smile, but his thin body was ram rod straight. Though he was much shorter than his wife, he seemed to be in command of the situation.

Helen made her eyes look at the other women as they entered. They wore dresses of the finest wools, satins, and velvets. These were women who were wealthy and knew they were secure and beautiful. Helen felt something inside of her shrivel. She had no money and no chance of getting any. She was here as a beggar and by the grace of God her aunt was willing to take her in. There was no way she could live up to those women's standards. Not even for a second son, let alone a first son who was heir to all their wealth.

Helen looked up and up. The tall man she had noticed stood besides her to be introduced. He was standing with another man, who seemed to be just as tall but a few years older. Helen was use to tall men, her folks and brother had been tall. So she looked up and they seemed so alike.

Aunt Clara said, "Helen, I want you to meet the Duke's sons. This is Henry his oldest son and heir and this is Edward the second son. He is going into the army I think, or was it the navy?" she laughed.

Henry bowed over her hand and gently kissed the tips of her fingers. Then Edward took hold of her hand. He turned her hand over and kissed the center of her palm. He smiled up at her.

"I hope to have the first waltz with you, or is your card filled.?"

Helen looked at the card at her wrist and smiled. "I never noticed it had to be filled. It is quite empty.'"

"Well then, you may put my name on your card. I would be honored if you let me dance more than one dance. Two would be fine, that is, if you wish to." Edward said as he laughed and his eyes shone on Helen.

Edward smiled into her eyes and moved on. Helen felt she was unable to breathe. Edward had made her feel so heavenly.

So-for the first time happy. She smoothed down the silver satin dress she was wearing. The dress was tight at the breast and waist, and then it spread out in yards of material. It had a bustle in the back that shook as she turned around to check it was still there. Then she smiled up at Aunt Grace, as she noted the lines of the invited guests had ended and she could leave this spot. Her Uncle nodded giving his approval that Helen should circulate.

"Have fun now," Aunt Grace said to her and moved into the crowd. Uncle Milton disappeared at the same time. Uncle Milton knew how to disappear at a party.

Helen stood where she was like a rooted tree. She didn't know what to do or where to go. She could feel the eyes of people staring at her. She could not stand like this all night. She had to move.

She felt someone take her shoulder and turn her around. It was Edward.

"You are the most lovely girl I have ever seen." Edward said as he stood in front of her.

Helen felt her face flush. She stared up at his eyes so gray. He gave a crooked smile and led her to the dance floor. He took her into his arms and Helen was swinging on a cloud of intense feelings of love.

"How nice of you to say that," said Helen as she stared at his big hands.

He grunted. He swung Helen into the music and dance. She could not believe that she was at a party again and enjoying it. She missed it so much, she did not realize how much she missed parties and dancing. Missed the conversation of flirting. She smiled up at Edward.

He looked down at her. His crooked smile showed his white teeth. He drew Helen closer to his body.

"May I call on you? " asked Edward.

Helen inclined her head. She was a plantation daughter who knew all the right moves to make. She knew how to flirt, it was a duty for all plantation women, but she didn't feel like flirting. She looked up at Edward and felt her heart beat faster. Was this the way her mother felt when she met Brad, Sr.? Her ears were ringing as she danced. She looked up at Edward and smiled.

"I would like that very much, if you called on me." she said.

"Then its settled. I have never seen a dream before, and you- you are a dream." whispered Edward. "I can not believe that you are real. You are what I dreamed about all my life."

Helen looked into the gray eyes of Edward. She smiled. She was so use to flirting and having men flirt with her. She knew she had come home again.

The night passed quickly. Helen danced and danced with several men who made no impression on her. She was so short Most men were short, compared to Edward. She danced with so many men, she could not keep track of it. She was surprised that there was so many short men in England. Perhaps she thought it was the air or fog that stunted their growth. Mostly she thought how tall Edward was. Would she see him again?

Dinner was served and several people took partners to enter the dining room. Edward pulled Helen's hand. "Come, we have to find a seat that is a little off from the other people. I want to get to know you."

Helen stared at him. Could a man that just saw her find her that attractive that he wanted to eat dinner with her? "Why would you want to eat with me. I'm sure you have many friends here."

Edward smiled his crooked smile. "Yes, but not one of them is as beautiful as you are. I want to claim you first so the rest will stay away. Do all women in the new world look as beautiful as you?"

Helen actually laughed. "No, this is something that is inherited by my family. Everyone of my family is tall, except that I am a throw back and short. I am the shrimp of the family. My mother was tall, and my father was even taller than you are. Is that what attracted you to me? That I am so small?"

Edward pulled her to a small dark blue velvet couch by the window. It was curved and the color seemed to make Helen stand out even more brilliantly. The silver dress sparkled as Helen stood by the couch. "Sit, I shall be your waiter and serve you. I want to hide you from the rest of this mob. For heavens sake, don't let some dolt take my seat. I know everyone wants to know you. You stand out in any crowd even if you are small and American. "

"I will watch your seat Edward. Are you sure you wish to serve me?" asked Helen

"More than a wish, I want to hide you forever, so you will be only mine." answered Edward.

"You say the nicest things, Edward." laughed Helen. "I feel so at home again. I can not believe how much I missed all this fun."

Helen felt her face burn red. She wished Edward really meant every word he said, because she felt so regal with him looking out for her. She wished she was rich and part of the ton, so he would love her. She knew the ton would not want her, if she was poor as she was. Only Lady Grace could save her vanity and her life.

Edward ambled off to the over loaded table to help himself with the food. He filled both plates with a little fish, some meat, Yorkshire pudding, green beans, and on each plate he put a slice of bread. He wasn't sure what Helen liked, but he tried a little of every thing on the table went into her plate.

Carrying the places back he looked at Helen. His heart did flip flops. He had looked and looked for a women he could love and never found one. And here he was, at a neighbors house, and to think that he almost did not go to the party. His brother had to talk him into coming so that he would not be alone. Here he found the women of his dreams. She was so beautiful. She was so slender. She was so lovely. It was hard to believe that he found the one women he had dreamed about right here. A woman he had dreamed about in his sleep and in his waking hours.

Edward handed her the plate he was carrying for her and sat down next to her. She smiled at him. "Why thank you. You are so thoughtful. I just adore all this lovely food. I haven't had any like this in ages."

Edward moved closer to her. "There are more things on the plate there than just food, I want you to notice, I put everything there was on your plate. I don't know what you like. But I want to learn. Would you like to take a ride tomorrow afternoon. I have some very fine horses that do need a run?"

"Yes, I just love horses. I grew up on a plantation in the South. As you know by now, we lost the war. We also lost our plantation. So maybe it is not so good an idea to become too friendly with me. I have no inheritance or anything you English look for."

Edward put a piece of meat into his mouth. He chewed it slowly. Then his storm grey eyes danced a merry tune. "Helen, my beautiful Helen, I am a second son. I have no great prospect. My brother will be the Duke. I shall go into the Navy or the army. Unless you hate that type of life. Would you like to go back to the new World? Or would the Army do you I can buy a commission. I would do anything for you."

Helen stared at him. Was she dreaming? She closed her eyes then opened them again to see if this was real life.

Edward put his hand on Helen's fingers. He could feel the cool touch of her skin. He looked into her eyes and he found himself reflected in their pools of blue. He felt like he could look into those eyes forever. His heart pounded, and he hoped that Helen felt something for him. He didn't want to rush things, but his time to go into the army was coming due very soon, and he felt if he let Helen go, he would lose everything that counted in life. His breath came in fits and starts, and he was afraid he would frighten Helen.

"Edward, you are so funny. I cannot believe you are real. We don't even know each other, and here you go - if I like the army, or go back to the South. No, I don't ever want to go back to the South. I hate it. I can never face the devastation that is there. I can not face the carpet baggers that are running the world I knew. No, Edward, I hope that I do not have to ever go back to the place of no hope and no dreams.."

Edward took her fingers and kissed them gently with his lips. He just did not ever want to let her go. He felt like fate was going to cheat him of his love.

When the evening ended and Edward held her hands in his. "You will go riding with me tomorrow afternoon?"

"Yes," whispered Helen as Edward bent and kissed her palm again.

The next day Helen and Edward went riding in his open carriage. Helen wore a dress of soft blue with ruffles around her neck and hem. The wind whispered in Helen's hair, but the little blue hat sat perkily at a tilt on Helen's head. Edward looked at Helen and they laughed and talked like old friends. Edward gently took Helen's hand into his large hand.

"I'm so afraid I will lose you Helen. You are the one I looked all over the world for, and I found you just next door."

"Edward, you say such nice things. I can listen to you all day and night." laughed Helen.

Edward's thumb stroked Helen's hand. Tremors went down her spine as she though of all the love that she could give and wanted to give. Her lake-blue eyes looked up at Edward's dark gray eyes. She smiled at him and he gave a crooked smile back.

"Look over there, see the apple tree in bloom. It's saying "Happy Season's Greeting.". Helen looked down at her hand held by Edward. His hand was so large and strong looking. Helen blushed as she thoughts of having him even closer than just his hand. She was old enough to be married. If not for the war, she would have been wed by now.

"What sort of Greeting are they giving?" asked Helen

"Greetings to us both," answered Edward. "saying Happy thoughts."

Edward took both his hands and turned Helen's face to his. He looked deeply into Helen's eyes. "Do you feel that extra pull in the air that tells you that we belong together?"

Helen blinked slowly as tears came to her eyes. She knew that Edward was the man whom she would always love. There would never be another like him. Yes, she would fellow him to the ends of the world.

"I can feel the pull on my arm, it is you Edward that have pulled my arm."

"Oh, Helen, You are so funny. You can feel we belong together, because we love each other. At least, I hope you love me." Edward looked at Helen with all the love which filled his eyes.

Helen looked down at her riding habit. She knew how she felt, she loved Edward.

Edward put his large hands under Helen's chin. He looked at her with his gray eyes gleaning with fire. "I love you Helen. I can say no more except I do love you."

"We do not know each other enough to Love," said Helen. Her heart pounded in her chest. She so wanted to be loved and loved by Edward, but she had no dowry and she had no hope of her life being better.

The Hopes, her aunt and uncle, made sure that Helen was invited to all the parties in the neighborhood. At many of the parties, she saw Edward, but he seemed to stay away from her. Then at other parties, he gave her so much attention it showed how much he loved her. It was so inconsistent.

One sunny day, an invitation came to go to Lord Wilson's small party but there was more, much more. Helen felt the excitement running through her veins. The Wilson's had invited her and Edward together. They both had invitations. Did that mean anything? She hoped it meant that people thought they belonged together. Yes, it was time she belonged to someone like Edward. Tall and strong, and so much taller than she was. He belonged to her family, tall and handsome, with blonde hair.

"Oh, Aunt Grace, I am so happy. Does that mean I shall lose my happiness as I have lost my home?" asked Helen "It seems every time I am happy, something happens to spoil it and I am adrift."

Aunt Grace shook her head. "No, It is time something good happened to you. You and Edward make a darling couple. I think even his mother agrees. I don't want you to worry about anything. That is why you have an Aunt and Uncle."

Helen looked up at Aunt Grace. "I hope that Edward's mother likes me, a little at least."

Edward picked her up in his closed carriage. He was surprised to see she was dressed in pure white, with white flowers in her golden hair. She even wore a white velvet evening cape. Her dress flowed to the floor like snow. It was without a bustle and swept with yards and yards of satin material. Her arms were bare but she wore white long gloves that covered her arms and hands. The dress was embroidered with white Lilly's encircling her bare neckline which outlined her white shoulders. Her neck rose above the dress like a swan. A snowflake of Lilly's lace covered most of her golden hair.

A carriage was all red and gold. She knew it belonged to the Duke, Edward's father, the Duke of York. Footmen stood at the back of the carriage. Each footman was dressed in red and gold. Those were the colors of the Duke of York. Edward handed Helen into the carriage as if she was the most delicate of flowers. His eyes twinkled at her as they sat back on the velvet seats.

"This should be a very nice party. Lord Wison always has the best music, and singers of anyone I know." said Edward "Plus did you notice, we are both invited as a couple. Helen, think of that bit for now. It means a great deal to me right now. It means people see us together, just as I do. Helen it is the best of times."

"Oh, Edward, I am looking forward to this party so much." Helen said. "I like the idea that they think of us as a couple I will think very much about that. In fact, that is all I thought about this week."

"Have you really thought of me? It means so much to me that you do." said Edward as he stared at Helen's face. "You know I leave in a week on active duty. I am going into the Army as I believe that would be best. For maybe us?"

Helen's heart pounded in her breast. Her mind whirled in ecstasy with the idea of living with Edward. How wonderful it would be. She would never have to see the old South and the devastation. She would forget her early life and think only the way it should be as only Edward and her were together. She brushed the bright lights in her mind, as she caressed the world and what could be possible if Edward really loved her as she loved him.

The carriage joined the line of carriages letting the guests off. Edward picked up Helen's hand and kissed it. He lingered over her hand as if he would never let it go. Helen gasped for air. It was so wonderful to know the evening had just begun. Their carriage came up to the front of the line and the footmen jumped down to let the step down and to open the door. Their gold braid shone in the candlelight. The candle light encased the whole mansion They stepped back as Edward nodded his head. He would do the honors of handing Helen from the steps and into his arms.

Edward exited first so he could help Helen down. He was not going to let the footmen touch his Helen. His, he wanted so badly to be his. He held Helen's hand and stared into her lake-blue eyes. She was his Dresden doll. He wanted her so much. Yet, he knew it was too soon to tell her. He did not want to frighten her away. Then he thought, how long should he wait to tell her he loved her? He must leave soon as his commission was about to happen. He had to tell her. He would not waste time waiting for the moment, he would tell her tonight. He would make her his tonight. He had to make sure she knew he loved her.

Helen felt her insides turn to water at his touch. She wanted him to know that she loved him with all her heart and soul. She knew it was time they said something to each other. She did not know how to make Edward ask her to be his wife. The glowing inside of Helen was about to explode. She wanted so much for him to love her. He lowered his face to hers and she experienced a sensation she had held back. Then he lifted his face and stared at her with an open heart. Her breath startled her as it came out of her mouth.

She tried to smile as they left the carriage and joined the crowd that led to the entrance of the mansion. The heaviness of the cape seemed to wrap around her body. It was too heavy to bare. She wanted to throw it off and stand ready to take on the world. Helen looked at Edward. Would he be ready to face the world with her? Was that what he wanted to tell her? Maybe, it was good-bye. She shook as the tears formed in her eyes. Helen looked at Edward from her lashes. She did not want him to know she was looking at him.

"Edward, I think it is time for us to talk. Maybe tomorrow, or the next day. But we must say what we feel for each other." Helen whispered as she looked down at the walk and wanted to sink into its depths as she said those words. Her fingers pleated the satin of her skirt.

"Helen, I have told you how I feel. So many times, in so many ways. But you are right. We have to talk. Tomorrow will be fine with me. How about us riding first?" Edward's heart beat on a rhythm of a native drum. He was so afraid that Helen would think that the time was too soon. He was running out of time. His commission was bought and he was to leave next week. He hardly knew Helen, but he knew he loved her with all his heart. The prick of his skin shot through his body as he touched her hand.

He looked down at the small hand he held so tightly. He loosened the hold of her hand and looked straight ahead.

They stood in line like everyone else. Helen glanced at Edward through her lashes. She did not want to scare him away. He held her hand in his, but to enable her to remove it if she desired.

The air smelled of the many different scents the ladies wore. The perfume rolled like waves of water. Everyone swayed to the breeze that blew softly through the trees that were lighted with candles. It was an enchanted evening. Everyone looked forward to the dancing and the singing that they knew their host would provide. Edward's thoughts lingered in his mind as he looked at Helen. She looked so small and fragile. He was not sure where he stood with her. He wanted to press her to his breast and love her with all his being. He did love Helen, but did she love him? There was only one way to find out, and find out he would. He tasted her lips without even having tasted them. He would tonight. He must. He knew her lips would taste like honey mixed with a spice of sugar.

The mansion glowed with candlelight in every room. It looked so warm and welcoming. They went up the curved steps to the mansion's wide open door. Helen and Edward stood in line as a footman introduced each new arrival. They stood face to face with their hosts and were introduced to Lord and Lady Wilson as if they had never met. After a few polite words they left the Wilson's for the next couple to be introduced. Together they came down the steps to the ballroom. The music was playing a waltz. Edward put his arms around Helen's waist and they glided over the dance floor. They twirled and whirled as one. Helen looked into Edwards eyes and they both were startled by the love they found there. Their hears pounded with the thought of being together forever. The dancers glided over the parquet wood floor. The colors of the many women's dresses whirled around and around in a frenzy of music.

Helen could feel the muscles of Edwards chest. They felt

so strong and secure. She wanted to stay near him forever. She smelled his smell of horses and leather and a small scent of apples. He must have eaten an apple recently. She pressed against his chest and she could feel his heart beat. They had known each other such a short time, and yet, she felt like she knew him forever. She loved his hands at her waist. He was so tall and big. Did he really like someone like her? Small and thin? In her heart of hearts she knew he belonged to her. She was secure in the knowledge that he did love her. She had to tell him that she did love him, without reservation, completely and forever.

The music stopped and Edward pulled Helen to the terrace. "Come:" was all he said as they trod into the grass. Edward pulled Helen into his arms. He could feel her warm body next to his. He felt his manhood straining against his trousers. He looked at Helen, and then bent his head down to hers. His lips touched Helen's lips like a breeze. He held her tighter and his mouth slammed down onto hers. He could feel the warmth of her lips. It was just like he thought, honey and sugar. He could not get enough of the love he felt for her. He made his tongue ride around her lips until she opened her mouth. He gently put his tongue into her mouth. He felt her shutter. They kissed. It was like heaven had descended to earth. They allowed the flow to spread through their bodies. His kiss teased and controlled her with passion. First the kiss was sweet and then, it grew bolder and rougher. It burnt into Helen's heart.

His large hands caressed her shoulders. Then he grew bolder and his hand went to her rear. He pulled her closer to his body. He could hardly wait till she was his and his alone. He did not think he had the courage to wait any longer. He wanted her and her alone. He was so sure she would let him do as he pleased. He noted a spot that held bushes that hid the bench behind it. It would be a perfect spot for his plans.

Helen never felt like this before. She felt her skin begin to burn. She pushed her body closer to Edward's body. She could not get enough of him. Hesitating a second she let her tongue go into his mouth and she felt him shiver. His hands went up to her breasts and he lightly touched the tips of her breasts.

Helen thought she would go out of her mind. She took a stilling breath as he looked down on her. She closed her eyes as she felt his hands once again on her breasts.

"Helen," Edward whispered, "look at me."

Helen looked up at him with her heart in her eyes. He looked down at her lake-blue eyes. Then he pulled her closer and kissed her again and again until her lips became puffed with his passion. He could not get enough of Helen. He needed the whole package her body, her mind, and her soul. He never wanted a woman; he never thought that he would want so desperately -Helen.

He looked once again at the bushes and the bench. He would take her there.

She would be his forever. She would have no choice in the matter. She would be his!

Edward took a deep breath. He knew he wanted Helen more than anything on earth, but it was too soon. He had never wanted any woman before, but when he looked at Helen, he could only see her laying next to him on satin sheets. He could picture her breasts all white with a pink topping like the apple blossoms. Her waist was so small his one hand wrapped around it. Her eyes spoke of love and his emotions ran ahead of his wishes. He could not wait forever; he could not wait any longer. He was stunned to think of what he was doing to Helen. He gulped and shook his head. What was wrong with him? He had to stop.

Edward took his hands off her body. He shook his head as the thought of what he was about to do to Helen. He looked down at her with all his heart open. "We better go inside. I think we have been out here too long as it is. Helen, please forgive me, if you feel I was too--"

Helen looked up at his face, and his smile was so crooked, "Please, don't talk about it. Not now. Edward."

"Promise me," said Edward, "that you will not give yourself to another. Please, promise me that. We -I- need time. I know you need time to adjust to our way of life."

Helen looked at him, "I promise to wait.," she said, "but I don't have the patience of a Saint. Edward, you have to --well all in due time I guess." She stopped and turned then walked into the doors leading into the dance floor.

Many men danced with her that night. Some so short she was embarrassed they asked her to dance. Some just as tall as she was. And only two that were taller than she.

Helen was far away in a dream world. She did not care or notice the men who danced with her. All her thoughts where for Edward. Did he mean what he said? Did he love her forever as she dreamed a love would be?

The time came when everyone started to leave. Edward came and fetched her to take her back in the carriage. He looked at her with brimming eyes of steel. "Remember your promise to wait for me, no matter what. You must remember. I love you."

Helen stared up into his eyes. She smiled a wide smile. "I shall always remember what you say, Edward. I shall always treasure whatever you say or want."

On the ride home, Edward had to remind himself to behave. He had to wait until Helen was ready. He was so ready. He wanted his lady now, right this moment, but he knew he had to wait till they talked.

He took her hand into his large hand and looked at how small and delicate it was. He saw her eyes flash with desire, that he held at bay. He could not think of anything to say to her other than to hold her hand. He was tongue tied. He never knew fear until he held her hand and thought of losing her. He never would let her go. She was his. She became his whole life. His reason for living and loving. She was all he cared about.

The next day, they went riding together. Edward was so shook up that he failed to notice that Helen was just as shaken as he was.

The chestnut horses pranced in their small space. They were saddled and ready to go. The horses were ready to fly but they stamped their feet and waited to their masters wish. Edward looked at the horses and his heart beat with the rhythm of their feet. He got on one horse and led the other horse to Helen's house.

The house looked so forbidden. It seemed to say nothing that Edward wanted would come true. He held his breath as he looked at the house. The house was the prison that his beautiful Helen lived in. He had to free her was all he thought about.

Edward called on her keeping the horses at his side. He jumped off his horse and tied the reins to the hitching post in front of the house. Helen glanced at Edward from the doorway of the house. She was wearing a green ridding habit of velvet. It encased her body tightly around her bust, but blossomed out at the waist. She smiled as she watched Edward dismount.

"I have been waiting for you," cried Helen as she laughed out loud.

"I could not sleep all night, thinking of our ride together. I have so much to say to you." Edward murmured.

Edward helped Helen mount her horse. Then he jumped on his horse. They looked at each other and smiled. Helen's dress draped over the horses rear. She shook her little green hat with the red feather and sat very still. She had the feeling that this was a point in her life that she could not miss. Time would tell. Her heart beat insanely as she looked at Edward.

She picked up the reins of the horse and they trotted out into the woods. The sparkling sun dappled and spun a web of gold. Helen looked at the beauty of nature and the warmth of the sun. The beauty of the world stood before her. Her blood ran smoothly through her being.

They went riding over the meadows and into the woods. They did not stop, but kept riding as if they were trying to out distance their feelings. Even though they had said they would talk about their feelings and such, they did not talk. The rode and rode.

During the week that followed, Edward was a wreck. They went to parties and danced together. Still when they danced, Edward made sure his body was far away from Helen's. He knew that his erection was evident to all who looked. He tried to hide his love. He wanted to love Helen so much. He even told his mother of his intentions of marrying Helen. His mother acted surprised as Edward had never shown any interest in any woman. Here he was telling her he wanted to marry Helen. She did not know what spell the woman held over her son. He was a loner and he seemed to detest any woman his brother brought home. When did he change? What made him change?

"Are you sure, Edward?" asked his mother, Regina.

"As sure as life is in me. I can not live without her. She is the only one that I will ever love," answered Edward. "I never looked at a girl before, but she is different."

"But you know her such a short time. It seems so strange to me," exclaimed his mother, Regina.

"The moment I saw her I knew she was the woman that I would marry and have children with. She is the only one I ever loved," said Edward

"Oh, Edward. If you are sure. Then I am all for it, as you will be in the Army this week, I do want you happy." said Edward's mother

"I shall be happy if Helen feels the slightest bit the same. Mother, I am so afraid that she will not love me, or not have me. What will I do?" questioned Edward.

"One thing you must remember, she is poor and has no money," said Regina in a royal voice.

"I don't care. It doesn't make and difference. We will be

in a the army. I have nothing I have to show off for," answered Edward.

"I do not like her, you might as well know that. She is a fortune hunter I am sure of that. She expects you to have money," said Regina.

"No mother, I told her we would have to live on my salary and she seemed perfectly happy. I only hope she excepts my offer of marriage. I am so frightened that she will not want to marry me." said Edward in a low voice as he looked at his mother.

Edward left his mother and got ready to look prosperous for Helen. He wanted her to see that the world would be wonderful once they were married.

Edward and Helen gathered energy from just being together, which they tried to hide from themselves, and from others. They would send shy glances at each other, but that was about as far as they went. They did not kiss again, nor did they try to be alone with each other. They just rode their horses in silence. It was like a war of endless passion tied to a tree and trying to break free.

Helen felt her heart beat faster every time Edward's name was just mentioned. She did not know what she should do to show him she wanted his kisses. It seemed that since she let him kiss her, he decided he did not want any more of her. Was she too wanton for him? Should she have stopped his touching her breasts and kissing her? It felt so right to let him touch her and to feel his manhood pushing to touch her body She cried in bed at night, wanting his touch, his love. Still he kept so far away from her.

It was time he became one with the Army. He was leaving that night. Edward urged her to step out in the garden with him. Helen looked at him., her lake-blue eyes watered. "Why should you want me to step into the garden now? You have ignored me for months. I feel like you wanted to never see me again."

They dismounted and looked at each other. The world turned around and around as Edward looked at Helen. He opened his mouth and found he could say nothing. He had to do it now, or never. He had to take his chances now, this moment in time. At first they stared at each other, then Edward stepped forward.

Edward looked at her. His stormy gray eyes took on a steel look. He ran his hands through his almost white gold hair. He gave a half smile and grabbed Helen by her arms. "You don't understand. I have nothing, nothing. My folks will pay for my way in the army, or send me to your new world. What have I to offer you? Would you be an officer's wife? I tried to talk my parents into giving me some land or a house, but they refuse. They say I should marry a rich woman. Helen, you are all I want."

Helen's heart beat faster and faster as she looked into his steel gray eyes. Edward leaned forward towards her face, but stopped inches from her lips.

"Edward, I would be an officer's wife of whatever, if we are together. I was so afraid you hated me for letting you kiss me. I thought you had lost all love for me. Oh, Edward, I don't care whatever happens will happen, just as long as we are together."

Edwards arms drew Helen to his chest. He kissed her with wild passion. He could not get enough of her. He had waited long enough. He was going to declare for her. He kissed her neck and her ear. He felt so elated that he could not believe his luck.

She trembled at his kissed and he could not stop. He wanted all of Helen. Now, and he would not wait for a preacher, his body burned. He put his hands on her rear and pulled her closer to his body. He could feel the tension disappear as he held her. The ocean that separated them was now lapping on the shore. They stood together and felt the passion of love.

"My mother thinks you are a fortune hunter," said Edward,

"but I don't know what fortune she is talking about. I have nothing as a second son. So we are even."

"Oh, Edward, I did want your mother to like me, let alone love me," said Helen with tears in her eyes.

"She will learn to love you. Who can't love you, my dear," said Edward as his hands roamed around Helen's body.

"My Aunt and Uncle will give me a small amount of money, not much, I can't accept a great deal. But it is nothing like a rich person will give you. Are you sure you want me?" asked Helen.

"You are the only one I have ever loved. You mean my life to me," said Edward as he stood away and looked at Helen.

They stood on the lawn outside the house of her Aunt and Uncle. The ride was over, but their hearts seemed to burst in their chests. The horses stood pawing the ground but happy to have stopped. They had a good ride. The sun was shining and the flowers were all in bloom. There was roses that filled the air with perfume. The colors vied with each other to see which was the most vibrant. Yellow and red, mixed with lavender and pale white seemed to fill the lawn. Edward pulled Helen close to him. He looked down on her and smiled. He wanted to pull her inside of him, but he could wait. He had to know how she felt. What if she did not want him. He would be devastated. He had never loved a woman like he loved Helen. She seemed to be his sun, his breath, his life.

"Helen, I want to marry you. I love you very much. I can ask your Uncle for you hand if you love me. Do you love me?" Edward looked at Helen with burning eyes.

Helen looked up at Edward. She loved every inch of him. She loved the way he smiled, that crooked smile. She loved his being so tall. He was tall like her family had been. She loved his tallness She loved how gentle he was with her. She would feel her heart beating double time every time he called on her. Life was so good to her. She felt that she never was so happy. She never thought she would find a man that would be taller than she was nor one that would love her as Edward loved her. Her hand went up to Edwards face. She brushed his cheek and then put her hand gently around his shoulder. "Oh, Edward, is this true? Is this really happening to us? I do love you Edward. I love you so very much. I would follow you to the ends of the world. There is nothing I would not do for you."

Edward pulled her close to his body. He could feel her warmth creeping into his body. "My love, I shall never love another as I love you>" He bent his head and kissed her gently on her mouth. Then he could not help himself, his kissed became filled with passion and want. His tongue shot into and out of Helen's mouth. His hand roamed around her slender body. He touched her breasts and he felt her breath.

He pulled her closer to his body. "I never thought I could love anyone as much as I love you. Oh, Helen. You make me want to turn cartwheels and sing."

Helen smiled her heart was in her eyes. She knew this was the finest moment of her life. This was all she wanted more than anything else on this earth. Edward was all she wanted. He was her life.

A high pitched cry was heard within the hall. Edward and Helen rushed in to see what was happening. Uncle Milton and Aunt Grace were standing next to Edwards mother who was crying..

"Mother," Edward rushed over to her, "what is the matter?"

His mother, Regina, the Duchess of York looked at him. Then he noticed his father was there also, and his younger sister. They all looked like they were beaten to death. They had a look of death. But it could not be, just when Edward was about to have what he desperately wanted.

The Duke walked over to Edward. He put his arms around Edward and leaned forward. The tears fell from his eyes. He hugged Edward tighter. "Your brother was out riding his horse. The horse tried to jump over a bush and got tangled in it. Your brother flew off the horse and broke his neck. Your brother is dead. You are now the heir to the Dukedom. I can't believe this happened. Your brother, trained to be the Duke now dead."

"No, not my brother, no. It could not happen like that. He was an excellent horseman." cried Edward. "He could jump over any hurdle. He was an excellent rider. He can not be dead."

The sadness crept into all their bones. There was a lost for words. No turning back the clock. The words written on the wind cried out to Edward. How could this happen to him? He who had the world in his hands. He who loved and cherished Helen.

Helen could feel the ice start in her veins. She knew what this meant. Edward could not marry her, no, under no circumstance. He had to marry someone with money and land but most of all, with a title.. She had nothing to give. Nothing at all. Edward was right for her as long as he was a second son, but a Duke, no, no, no. She knew without being told that Regina, Edwards mother, would be glad this happened as she despised Helen. No, she loved the oldest son, she would not be glad. Helen was like a fly that would leave and never to heard of again.

She listened to his mother. "You have to act like a Duke now. You can not go into the navy or army. You have to marry someone with a title. Some one who has money and is part of the ton. You have to uphold your position. You are not free any longer. You have to act and do as a Duke."

"No mother," shouted Edward, "I told you I am going to marry Helen."

"You must act like a Duke. You have an obligation now for the future of your children and your heirs." said his mother in a whisper.

Edward's shoulders slumped. He did not know what to say or do with his brother's death. He knew he had to go home to take care of his brother, and he had to love his mother and father as he was all they had as sons. Did he have to give up Helen? He knew he could not, and yet, he was so brought up to respect the old ways. He felt like he could hardly breath. He had his duty and he had his heart. What was the most important thing to do?

She watched them take Edward into their carriage. She watched as they left. She watched until the carriage was out of sight. She ran up to her room and flung herself onto her bed. The tears fell against the silk cover. She almost had it all. She looked around her room. It felt so strange suddenly with it all done in soft blues and whites. She knew she could not stay here forever. She knew that when she came. But she had hopes of marrying someone here in England. Now, no matter what, she would never marry If she could not have Edward, what was her life. It was a lie for her to even live.

She heard the soft tapping on her door. She did not want to answer it, but she knew she was obligated to answer her Aunt Grace no matter how she felt. She wiped her eyes on her sleeve of her dress. She almost had it all. She slid off the bed and went to the door. She opened it and stared into her Aunt Grace's eyes.

"Helen, are you all right?" asked Aunt Grace

"No, yes, Oh, Aunt Grace," cried Helen.

"You realize that you and Edward are ended. He is to be the Duke. I am afraid even with the dowry we will give you, it would not be enough. He will need land, and money and he must marry someone with a title.. He is to be The Duke."

"Oh, Aunt Grace, what shall I do?" Helen wrapped her arms around her aunt.

Aunt Grace patted her back. "Why not wait to see what will happen? It seems he is rich beyond belief. It may not matter money and land. And we shall give you money. Maybe it will be enough."

"Nothing will be enough for Edward's mother. She never liked me. She is glad in her heart that I am finished. I am dead.

There is no reason for me to live. Every thing I had turned to dust. I am unlucky."

Helen looked into Aunt Grace's eyes. Helen squeezed her eyes shut. She really had very little hope, but still a small flame burnt in her heart. She loved Edward so very much, and she just could not believe that she had lost him. NO, she would wait and see what would happen.

The week past so slowly. The funeral was solemn. They buried Edward's brother with all the pomp and glory that was due a duke's son. Sadness invaded the house of the Duke. No callers were admitted after the burial. It was like the world had ended. Regina, Edward's mother, saw no one. She was lost in a grief so bitter it went through her veins and into her heart. She would not believe her son was dead.

Another week sailed by, and Helen had lost weight, waiting to hear something, anything from Edward. All was still. Nothing was said, no letter sent. A void entered Helen's heart. She understood. Edward was in another world than she was. He was to learn the world of the Duke. He lived in a different world than Helen.

On the third week, The Duchess of York called on the house of Lord and Lady Hope. The Duchess was wearing black. Her hat was covered with veils as was her face.

Aunt Grace met her and greeted her. She led her into the sitting room filled with velvet settees and chairs. The walnut tables gleamed in the light. The candles cast shadows across the room and the fire in the fire place blazed. Aunt Grace told the butler to bring in tea.

"Won't you please sit?" asked Aunt Grace

The Duchess sat. "I really want to see your niece Helen. I want her to go on home to the new world. I don't want her near Edward. He had enough on his plate."

The Duchess pulled aside her veils and stared at Aunt Grace.

Aunt Grace watched as the maid brought in the tea. The

maid wore a black dress with a white frilly apron over it. The maid poured the tea for the two ladies. There were tiny sandwiches on the tray and an assortment of small cakes.

Aunt Grace handed the Duchess the tea. The Duchess looked down into the liquid, "I must speak to Helen alone. Do you mind.? I have to have her understand that Edward and she are finished. She should go back to where she belongs. She is not part of our life."

Aunt Grace put her tea down. "Yes, I do mind. If you have something to say to Helen, I would like to be present." Aunt Grace pulled her hands into her lap. Her morning dress was a soft green with lace ruffles around her neck. Aunt Grace's long fingers touched her ruffles on her neck. She was upset, because she knew what the Duchess was about to say to Helen.

"Very well, if that is what you wish. Will you send for Helen now?" asked Regina.

Aunt Grace looked at the Duchess whose white face showed little emotion. Aunt Grace rang the bell that was next to her. The same maid that brought the tea in, answered the bell. "Yes Mum."

"Please ask Miss Helen to come into the sitting room," Aunt Grace said as her fingers once again went into her lap and grasped the other hand.

The maid left. The Duchess and Aunt Grace sat very still. The duchess put her tea on the tray. The silence was like thunder. Finally a soft knock was tapped on the door.

"Come in, "said Aunt Grace as she turned to watch Helen enter. Helen was wearing a soft yellow dress filled with embroidered flower in red and green. Helen stopped short. She saw the Duchess. Then she came forward. Aunt Grace motioned her to sit on a chair near were they were sitting. Helen knew what Regina was going to say. Her world was tipsy. There was nothing left for Helen.

"The Duchess wanted to talk to you alone, but I thought it would be better if I stayed. Do you want me to leave?"

asked Aunt Grace "We both know what the Duchess has to say."

"No," cried Helen. Her heart stopped beating, her head hurt, she wanted to die. So Edward didn't have the nerve to face her. "No, NO." she cried again.

The Duchess fiddled with her veil, pushing it further back. Her pale face held no expression. "I might as well get to the point. I do not want you near Edward. He will be the Duke. You have nothing to offer him. It would be better if you went back to the new world and your brother. Can I say it any blunter? Of course, I shall be paying your way back there. In fact, if you feel I should pay you some extra money, then I shall gladly do it to be rid of you."

Aunt Grace stood up. "I can afford to pay for the passage to the New World, for Helen if I want her to go. You have no right to dictate to me or her where she should go. You may be a wife of the Duke, but we still live in a land where there is choice. I choose to keep Helen here. What have you to say to that?"

"Nothing," said the Duchess. "Helen knows her duty. I am sure she knows Edward will be out of reach for her. Is there anything else to say?"

The Duchess stood up and pushed against the table that held the tea tray, cakes, and cups and sauces. The table wobbled. and then fell. It crashed to the rug. The china broke, and the silver tea pot lay on its side seeping out tea. The rug slurped up the spilled liquid. The maid stared in horror. The rug wet with the water from the tea pot seemed content.

The Duchess's face turned red. "Well, then, do as you like. But Edward is out of bounds for Helen. I don't want her at parties that Edward will be looking for a proper wife. If she stays, just keep her away from Edward."

Helen shook as she took in the scene. The two women glared at each other. The Duchess bunched up her hands into fists. Her black lace gloves seemed ready to hit some one. Aunt

Grace snarled. "Helen will be with me forever and if she is invited to parties, she will go. I will not have you dictate to me what she will do."

The Duchess turned her back and walked out of the room and out the front door. Helen felt the tears falling from her eyes. Aunt Grace looked at Helen and pulled her into her arms. Helen cried and cried against Aunt Grace's shoulder. Helen felt her heart split into pieces. The maid gathered up the broken pieces of china and set the tea pot to rights. It seemed an impossible task, but the maid looked at Helen, and knew this was nothing compared to what Helen felt.

"There is no reason for me to stay here, Aunt Grace," Helen said finally as she looked into her Aunt's eyes. "I will go to Brad and live with him. There is nothing left for me here. I shall never marry. I loved Edward so. There is no reason for me to stay any more. Please forgive me Aunt Grace, but I want to go back to the new world. Staying here is death."

Aunt Grace shook her head. She understood. There was nothing left for Helen. Aunt Grace kissed Helen on her cheek. She held her tight in her arms.

"Oh, child, I love you so. You are the child I never had. What will become of you? There is no plantation to go back to. There is nothing left in your world and no, I am afraid there is nothing left in Edward's world. He had to act like a Duke. He had tradition to follow. He has no choice."

Helen moved away from Aunt Grace. "Aunt Grace, you must understand. I had something no one can take away from me. I love Edward, and will always love him. But it is impossible for us to be together. I love him so much, I can not be here in England. He has to find a wife to suit his status. He has to live up to being a duke. It was alright when he was a second son, but now, now.--"

Helen walked over to the window and pulled the long dark purple drapes and looked out at the garden. It was in this very garden Edward asked her to marry him. It was were Edward had proposed to her. It was a sacred spot. But it was a place she should not, could not, not ever, go there again.

"I must go back to the new world again. The sooner I go the better it will be for everyone. Aunt Grace. You have to just understand, I can not stay here any longer."

Aunt Grace felt the tears stream down her face. "I wanted so much to have you but it is best if you go. Your heart will mend. You are young. You have to believe that you will mend. You will write me, you will remember me?"

Helen turned to the doorway. "I shall pack. We better send a telegram to Brad. Bet he will be surprised to see me again. Of course, I will write you. But I will have so little to say. What will I do when Brad learns I am coming back? Will he forgive me that I have returned? I wonder what I shall do. He was so proud of the money he had to send me to England. Now what will he think?"

Helen walked up the staircase bent like an old woman. Her dreams had been shattered and so had her heart. Edward had to live a life that was meant for a duke, and she had to live a life meant for someone without any hope. Her plantation gone, her hopes of love gone, and Brad, her brother, how will he feel to see her again? Will he strangle her now? No. He was a family man, so he will take her back, but under duress.

As she reached her room, she could feel the strong arms of Edward encircling her waist. She felt his kisses on her lips, dew drops of despair hit her. She bent over double and the tears dripped from her eyes. She must be brave and forget that once she had love.

She pulled out her old plantation dresses with a hoop that went under the skirt. She would take nothing that she did not bring with her. The hoop was all bent out of shape. There was nothing for her to do but hold up her dresses as she walked. The dress was too long without the hoop. She would not take the dresses her Aunt made for her. She wanted no reminders of what had been and what might have been. She loved Edward with all her heart and being. She could not want anything else in her life. She was betrayed by the English law to marry the rich Ton. She was not rich, or pretended to be. She was a lost soul.

There was nothing she had to live for. What does it matter if she never married? No one cared what she did. Brad thought she was safe in England. What a surprise to find her back in the new world How could she support herself? Should she just end it all before she reached Brad? She had to think about this long and hard. Edward was lost to her forever. Her heart was dead.

Was the only way to support herself to marry? Would she have children? What was she thinking? Would she go back and see what was going to happen to Edward and London? How could she. Their world was over, there was nothing left to it. Would she have the nerve to see who Edward married? If things looked bleak as they did now, she would kill herself. She had no reason to live. Could she live with Brad, her brother again? He was a gambler, and what would she do?

Chapter IX

CLAIRESS AND McGUIRE CANTERED ALONG the river towards New Orleans. McQuire's face was tense. He was worried how Helen had made out with him gone. He just knew in his bones something bad happened to her. Who would look after her, she was so innocent. When he met her, Helen's eyes were dead. He had to find a way to make her alive again. Whatever happened while she was in England had changed her life for good.

Clairese nestled into his body. She just knew that he was thinking of something else, he was not here. She had to awaken him to the dangers that lurked near them. She was responsible for their predicament. How could she make it up to McGuire? She rubbed her rear into McGuire's body.

"Wake up," said Clairese. "It is time to think of the horses and the guys on the other side of the river. We are not home free yet. We have left the pack horse behind, and we have enough food for a day. That is it. So start thinking of the here and now. You can not change anything till we get to New Orleans."

"How did you know I was thinking of New Orleans?" asked McGuire.

"It's easy," said Clairese, "you have that far away look in your drawn to be forever eyes."

Clarisse's brown curly hair fell around her face and lifted with the movement of the horse. She shook her head. How in the world was she going to make McGuire see that she wanted him so very much. Every time she looked at him her heart pounded like stones rubbing against each other. He was so much a man. A real man to love and trust, and she had to make him see she could help him.

Clairess turned her head and looked at McGuire. "I think some how, the Odge brothers must keep track of the half breed and the German."

"We're making good time, I don't think they will be any trouble to us. We are on the horses, so there is no stopping us."

"McGuire, I just have this odd feeling, that this is too easy. There must be something we have overlooked," said Clairess as she caressed the horse they both rode. "The brothers are the best trackers in the world. I know they hated the German and the Indian but they had to have some way to keep track of each other. LaCount would have it so. He leaves nothing to chance. He thinks out each move like a chess game."

"What's there to worry about?" asked McGuire. "We are on a horse, and nothing can stop us now."

"I have this feeling that something is wrong," said Clairese.

"I admit we have to rest this horse, but we can change to the other horse, and we are on our way. Don't worry that you have to ride with me. We are still making good time. Much better than walking in this mud."

"If you think it is O.K. then I will also. But we should think of those other men. They are said to be the best trackers in the world." said Clairese as she shook he head. Her hair flew in all directions. She needed a comb. Or something to make her hair look decent. Yet, she was not free. She had this strange feeling that they were going to regret not looking around now.

McGuire laughed, and at that second a wet net settled on him, and his horse. He was shocked at first but he quickly pulled out his gun from his pants. He pointed the gun from the point the net had come from.

The wet net curled around McGuire like a snake. He could smell the waters of the Mississippi River in each fold. He looked at Clairese and found the net did not cover her. He was surprised at this as Clairese was just in front of him. He touched the net and felt it draw closer to his body. His gun only had one shot. It did not hold more than that. McGuire knew he was a crack shot, but still, he was covered by a net that was being pulled tighter and tighter around his body.

He stared up the tree and he saw Tom Odge laughing out loud. He could see Tom's yellow teeth and his huge nose. McGuire pointed his gun at Tom and fired through the net. Tom looked startled. He grabbed his fat chest. His bloated face turned red with anger. His ears swayed as he fell out of the tree. He lay before the netted horse and riders like a bloated whale. He shook, gasped for air and just as suddenly he lay still. Amos and Phil stared at McGuire. McGuire had killed their brother. They could not believe something like this happened to them. They never had anyone shot at them. In fact, everyone was afraid of them. They were the Odge brothers!

Amos Odge screamed. "You son of a bitch," He lifted his revolver and took aim. McGuire could do nothing with his gun as it was a one shot gun. Amos fired at McGuire. McGuire felt the hot bullet enter his side. He bent double over the saddle and the net drew tighter around the front of him and his horse. The net did not cover Clairese. She was free of the net. McGuire felt weak as he held his side. With a last effort, he cried out, "Jump, Clairese jump and run. Don't let these devils get you. Clairese, run. Don't look back.".

The net was near her, but did not cover her. She shrugged her shoulders. She must flee. She could not stay here like a butterfly caught on fly paper. But for a second, she could not think or move. She was like a statue that was held in place by a stone of unknown origin.

Clairese bent over the front of their horse and jumped off. She was free of the net. Her body double over. Then, she just ran. She ran as if the demon LaCount was after her. She did not look back as McGuire had said. She knew her life was at an end if she stopped. She shot into the woods near the road. She felt the tears run down her face. McGuire was surely going to die. If he died there was no way that she wanted to live.

She almost turned and gave herself up. But then she thought, I have to help McGuire if he is alive. What if he is dead? I have nothing left to live for. He gave me hope. All I have left is that I help him somehow and some way.

I can do it, thought Clairese, I can save him somehow. I will do it, or die trying.

The two Odge brothers watched her go. Phil laughed "Hell, we'll find her easy. We are the best trackers there is, no hiding from us. We will catch up to her later. Right now we're gong to torture McGuire for killing our brother. No one messes with the Odge brothers. I want to hear him scream for mercy. I want him to gravel in the dirt. I want him dead."

"LaCount wants him dead. We have to kill him quickly and then we have to kill Clairese. He does not want them to complicate his life. We better do as he says." said Phil. "No sense getting on the bad side of LaCount."

"No one tells me what to do, least of all LaCount. Who does he think he is? A horse's ass if you ask me. We are the best, that is why he hired us. We do what we please." said Amos.

Phil looked at Amos. "You're not afraid of LaCount? I am petrified by him. He can do anything to any one he wants to. He is not to be fooled with. What is wrong with you Amos?"

Amos looked at Phil. "I can't believe you. Are you really a man or a mouse?"

Phil looked down at his dead brother. His body shook with sorrow. He just could not believe that his brother was dead and McGuire lived. "I don't know any more. I just feel lets get this job over with and head back home."

"Never," said Amos. "We are going to torture this man and then get Clairese and have her, and then kill her. I have made up my mind. No one is going to change it, especially you, Phil."

There was no sense having an argument with Amos. Once he made up his mind it was what he would do come hell or high water.

They dragged McGuire out of the net and bound his hands and feet. He lay quietly on the mud because he was frozen in time. The bullet hole in his side bleed freely. He then passed out from the loss of blood.

Phil, the short squat brother, started to build a fire. "Bet you wonder how we knew something happened to the old Indian and German." Phil waited, but McGuire did not say anything. McGuire lay still. Phil looked at McGuire. He saw McGuire was unconscious. Phil wanted to laugh. Wait till he had the fire built, then McGuire would not have such a pretty face anymore. He was going to burn that too good looking face. He was always jealous of McGuire's good looks. He was going to fix that. Then he looked at Amos. Amos was ready to torture, but he could care less about his face. It was his body that Amos wanted to destroy.

Phil gave a shrill laugh. He knew no one was listening to him, but he wanted to talk and tell how clever they were. "Well, anyway, I'll tell you. They were told by LaCount how we were to keep in touch witch each other. That was by fire. A certain way the fire was to be build. When they didn't build the fire the way we agreed, in fact there was no fire, we knew something happened to them. Hey, we didn't like them either, but that don't make us brothers. So we jumped in the boat, and surprise, we saw you get the horses. Easy way to get you was to use the net we found in the boat, as it was a fishing boat we borrowed. Ha, Ha. And used it. On McGuire."

Amos walked over. His shadow cast over McGuire. He was tall, with broad muscular shoulders. He had a sneer on his face.

"You talk too much Phil. Your mouth runs away with you, and no one listens to you. How the hell would anyone listen to you when you ramble. McGuire should be waken up so we can torture him and kill him. I don't want to take too long here. There are girls waiting for me back in New Orleans."

"Since when do you have girls waiting for you? You think your great?" asked Phil

"A lot you know." Amos answered "I have lots of women. They love me."

Phil laughed at Amos. "You're dreaming, old sod. You are no LaCount."

"Why do you always bring up LaCount? Wish you would forget him for a time. I find him a terror, but I never think of him." said Amos

"Yeah, right. Like I never think of raping Clairese before we kill her. She is one hot pepper." said Phil. Phil filled his mouth with spit.

Phil swallowed his spit. He wanted to spit on McGuire but some how he knew Amos would be mad because it would accomplish nothing. Amos was the leader and he expected everyone to listen to him. He did not waste a motion; he did what he wanted and then he was happy.

Phil looked at his brother Amos and nodded. Phil was not one to make Amos angry. "Just building the fire to burn that pretty face of McQuire's. Just talking to kill the time. I like to talk I guess, even if it is to myself. Sort of brag."

Amos looked around. No one was near. "We'll get the girl later. No rush. She has no place to go, except New Orleans, so we don't even have to track her."

"What if a snake gets her?"

"So what, we have to kill her"

"But I thought we should have some fun with her. You know, what I mean-"

Phil shook. He rattled his body as the first flames of the fire started to glow. "Orders are to get rid of McGuire forever.

But Amos, he didn't say we can't have fun and torture him first. I mean-"

Amos looked at Phil. "If you want the fun, then take it. In fact, I'll help you. Always hated this handsome bastard. He walks around like he owns the world. And all the girls turn cart wheels where ever he goes."

McGuire started to wake up. He felt his hands tied tightly. They were getting numb. His legs were tied just as tight, and he could feel the blood rushing to flow down there. He knew he was a goner. One way or the other, he had a bullet in his side, and torture from the Ogden brothers to look forward to. Not much to look forward to, and no one to save him. He hoped the Clairese had at least gotten away and was smart enough to chuck the horse and swing from tree to tree. Those ugly brothers would use her till she died.

McGuire felt that everything he ever tried to do ended in failure. Lost the war, lost the plantation, and now he lost Helen. His life was a big loser, but he sure hated not being there for Helen.

He heard the Ogden brothers stirring up the fire. Now they were bickering over what type of stick they needed to brand his face with. What difference did it make, he wondered. He would be dead one way or another. Probably the bullet that was lodged in his side would do him in. Not much time to think of things like that. Sort of make his peace with God he thought. Sorry I was such a loser he prayed.

"Ah, come on Phil, lets burn him all over. Especially his love making parts. He is known as a Romeo. So lets get rid of that first."

"Anything you say, Amos," Phil said as he walked further from the fire and into the woods looking for a stick. He heard a strange sound. Like a wild turkey might make. He turned his head. A stump slammed into his face and he fell down. Then the stump was dropped and a thin knife plunged into his heart. Phil was dead before he could yell a warning.

Clairese large black-gray eyes blinked. Her honey colored skin was sprinkled by the light of the sun and tree leaves. She looked at the blood that covered the knife. She heaved a sigh as her large breasts shook. She had to save McGuire, and Amos was left there, big and strong, and smart. She watched the blood spurt as she pulled the knife from Phil's chest. Blood covered the front of her chemise.

Amos yelled "Phil, where the hell are you Phil?"

Only silence echoed back silence. Amos looked at McGuire. "Well you can't go any where, Where did that dumb brother of mine go to? I better go look for him. Bet he got stuck in some mud or bog. Always was a fool."

Amos ambled into the trees. Clairese watched him go. Silently she slipped out of the trees and ran to McGuire. She quickly cut the ropes around McQuire's hands and feet. with her bloody knife. She shook him. "Quick, get up, Quick."

McGuire stretched his long frame. Clairese handed him a loaded gun. "Come on, you have to kill that Amos. Right now. You hear, or Lord, look he is coming back. McGuire move, do something. Take the gun."

McGuire slowly moved his hands and feet, He tried to sit up, but the blood did not circulate in his feet or arms. He lay still as someone dead. Amos came out of the woods. He saw Clairese and he saw McGuire laying so still. .

"Well, Hell, I don't even have to look for you. You fall for this handsome fellow? Ha, next time, you see him, he be a charcoal. Ha. I always had a taste for you, but LaCount had you first, so-""

Amos rushed over to Clairese, but Clairese started to run towards the Mississippi. McGuire moved his body and thrust out the gun. He had one shot at Amos, and it had to be good or both he and Clairese would be dead.

Slowly as he watched Amos run towards Clairese he raised his gun. Slowly he took aim. The days of the war entered into his head, He was back in the war. He could hear the cannons roar. He watched the Union soldier starting to kill his friends. He had to protect his friends. He pulled the gun up to a position to shoot. He, McGuire squeezed the trigger. Amos clutched his chest. He stumbled to his knees. Amos let out a loud bellow. He staggered, and fell to his knees. He tried to get up, but then he fell to the ground. He did not move.

Clairese stood near the river bank. She watched Amos as in a trance. She took a step forward, and then she hesitated. Could he be dead, really dead? No., No. It was too easy.

McGuire shook his head. The war was over. He was in the mud of the Mississippi. He just killed a man. Why?? Then it all came back to him. The hunt, the brothers, the fire, and Helen. McGuire finally managed to get up from the ground. He was very shaky, but he held the pistol by the butt. He slowly walked over to Amos. He knew the pistol held no more bullets, it was only one shot, but the gun could be a weapon if he need it.

He reached Amos and bent down. Amos was dead. There was no doubt about that. He lay, not moving, with his large hands over his heart. McGuire felt his pulse. He had no pulse.

McGuire looked at Clairese, "Do you know where Phil is?"

"I killed him," Clairese said as she came back to McQuire's side. She looked at McGuire. The blood ran rapidly out of his side. "I have to bind your side or you will die for want of blood."

McGuire looked down at his side. He felt his head swim. He sat down abruptly.. Clairese pulled the shirt from Amos. She made long strips of the shirt with her knife.

"This might hurt," she said to McGuire. She probed for the bullet with her finger. She felt nothing. Then she took her knife and probed. Ah, she felt the bullet, embedded in McQuire's side. Clairese looked around. She spied a pot the Ogden brothers had brought in with their supplies. She picked it up. and filled it with water. She put the pot of water over the fire to boil.

"I have to get the bullet out, before it poisons you. It will hurt. I will try to be as fast as I can. I have done this before. Wait, see the Ogden brothers brought whiskey with them Good. Now you can drink it some down, and I can use some of it to sterilize your side."

McGuire drank the whiskey. Clairese poured some whiskey on his side. It burnt like holy hell. McGuire did not scream, just sat there and watched Clairese. She took her knife and gently probed the bullet from his side. She put the shirt strips in boiling water, and then wrung them out. She returned them to the boiling water. Then she carefully held them by the edge and put them on McQuire's side. He yelled "My god woman, what are you doing?"

"This will stop an infection. Now lay down and rest. We can not go any where till tomorrow. You want to help Helen, then you better be in shape to do so." said Clairese.

McGuire lay down. His eyes closed. He slept. Clairese looked at him and smiled. "Come into my parlor, said the spider to the fly," Then Clairese laughed and laughed. She was going to have exactly what she wanted and there was no stopping her. She laid down next to McGuire and put her hands around his body. She would protect him with her life.

The moon came up and sparkled on the water. Clairese still lay next to McGuire with her hands around him, holding him She felt McGuire stir. She pressed her lips on his mouth. She felt the warmth of his mouth move. She kissed him slowly

Her small tongue roamed around his mouth. She felt him stir. She pulled her closer and he kissed her with a wonton air. His mouth closed hungrily over hers. She pushed even closer. McGuire opened his eyes. He looked into her smoky black-gray eyes. Her eyes were like lightning bolts of desire. McGuire knew he was lost. He had to have the whole of this woman.

He pulled off his clothing and boots. He pulled off her clothing. They lay there naked. The mud felt like a feather bed. He smiled at her. His hands caressed her back. The skin felt like a mixture of sand and sun and lust.. He pulled her closer still. She could feel his awakening below. She pushed herself against his manhood.

He leaned down and suckled her breast. Then he played with the other breast. Her hands went into his hair and ran back and forth for awhile. Then her hands went down his back. He suckled the other breast and moaned.

"Oh, Clairese, I did want you so badly, but I am afraid. Every woman I really wanted leaves. me. Please say you that you will never leave me. I need you;."

"I'll never leave you, McGuire. Only death can part us. I love you so. I never knew what love was all about till now. I was with LaCount, but I was only 18 when he took me. He liked them young, I think.. McGuire love me, fill me, do what you want with me. I am yours."

McGuire slowly entered her. He could feel the warmth of her encircle his manhood. He knew that this time he had the valuable gift of love. It was something he had looked for a long time. They lost track of time. It seemed that there was so much feelings to be considered that time stood still. Clairese moaned as they swayed together. McGuire was surprised at his response. He felt like he never had really loved before. Clairese struggled with her breath as she felt like she had reached heaven. Could love be so wonderful and fulfilling?

Finally they lay in each others arms without moving. McGuire looked at Clairese. "You know, we can go to Texas and start all over. I got enough money to buy a farm or horse ranch. We can get married, have children, all the dreams, I have always held."

"McGuire, do you mean you would marry me? Really? I can't believe that you would want me, after I was mistress to LaCount for so many years. Wasted years".

"Clairese, what does it matter the past, it is the present we must think about. Yes, I want to marry you, but please, call me Brad. That is my name."

Clairese pulled McGuire closer and kissed him hard and earnest. Tears streamed down her eyes. She was so happy, she could not believe that this was happening to her. Her, who always had to bend the knee to others. Clairese who always had to mind her mouth and be pleasant and sweet.

McGuire took his handkerchief and blotted her eyes. She smiled at him. He hugged her and said. "Say, we better get going and get my sister. Will she be surprised that we ware going to Texas."

"Will you sister mind me being with you? You know, I'm not a whity" said Clairese

"No, I think she will be happy I found someone." answered McGuire as he stood up and dressed. "But we do have to hurry to New Orleans and get Helen."

Clairese smiled. She had never known what happiness was until this moment She looked at McGuire and her heart beat wildly inside her body. She was going to have a husband, a home, and children. What she always wanted. Someone who loved her, and someone she could love. Life was great at the moment. It held all her dreams wrapped around a big great heart of McGuire.

Clairese jumped up from the ground and started to dress. They would be in New Orleans in no time. Then they would go to Texas. As Clairese strapped her knife against her side she could not believe her good fortune. She had never been lucky. Her grandmother sold her to LaCount when she was 18 years old, and that was all she knew. Still, she had dreams, dreams of love, and family. Clarese pushed her curly brown hair in back of her head..

'Come on McGuire," She laughed, "Time is wasting. Let's get your sister, and let's get out of this wilderness." Clairese ran to the horses and brought them to McGuire.

"You know, I always wanted a horse farm," said McGuire

"Darling, I want just a home and family, and most important of all, I want you."

Chapter X

A WAS AS BLACK AS the wood that he used to build his one room shack. He was a Skelton and slightly stooped. His only food was what Nellie brought to him once so often. He shook his large head. Once, he was a strong solid man. He had a woman, that was Nellie, that brought him food, but went on to find a strong healthy man. Nellie worked long hours house cleaning and stealing food. Food was hard to get. Nellie remembered that they had at daughter who they called Louise. Louise had left so long ago it was to believe that she was part of him, Jim. Jim was the only name he had. It was an outstanding name when he was young and strong. But now, he just existed.

He remembered the last time he saw Louise. She came into his shack and just stared at him.

"I'm pregnant, and I'm too far gone to have an abortion. I have to have this kid, but I'll not keep it. If you want the kid it's yours." said Louise as she lowered her big stomach on the bed.

Jim looked at her. "How come you having a kid?"

"Knocked up in the whore house. You know. I was drunk as a lute for the past few months. So I have to pay for it. Tried to have abortion but the abortionist would not do it."

"Come on Louise, an abortionist would do it if you paid."

Jim strode around the room. "Did you come here for money. I don't have any."

"You never have anything." pouted Louise. "why do I bother coming here?"

"To strut your stuff." replied Jim

The small room had one door, a window, a bed and a broken chair. Other than that there was a bucket for water and a table that sat crooked in the corner.

Jim wanted to sit down, but the only place to sit was on the bed, and Louise was on the bed. He sure didn't want to sit with her.

Louise tugged at her breast. She was uncomfortable, and she hated her parents. She could hardly run fast enough to become a whore in the whorehouse that catered to white men. She lowered her eyes that were dark brown. She once was a beautiful girl, but things had changed. She was wrung out; she was thin as a rail except for her protruding stomach.

"What can I do Pa?" asked Louise.

"Well, have the kid and then see." replied Jim

"I'm going to dump it in the garbage can." cried Louise

"Your flesh and blood?" asked Jim

"What can I do with a kid? I was thrown out of the whorehouse because they can't use me now. What am I going to do? Where is Nellie? She will help me." said Louise.

"Nellie found a strong man to live with. She'll not help you. She bring me food now and then. That's how I'm alive in the here and now." said Jim as he leaned against the wooden slats of his house. It was hard to see the difference between the wall and Jim. He blended into the dark old black wood.

"No way I'm going to keep this kid, whatever it is," cried Louise

"Can't keep myself alive, let alone a kid," said Jim slowly He looked out the one window and he could see the rest of the shacks like his. This was not a rich place to live. All the old wood was used for shelter. Some of the houses were made of paper. Not much chance for life. The paper fell apart during the rain, and it rained a great deal in New Orleans.

"Can I stay here?" asked Louise

"I only have one bed," said Jim

"I'll sleep on the floor. You have the cleanest place around. No rats. I can get another blanket." pleaded Louise

Jim felt his heart break. Clean because he had no food. Always clean! He was tired of clean. He wished he had a whole ham. Maybe grits! Sweet potatoes, and black eyes peas! "You can stay, but on the floor. I'm not giving up my bed for you. You ran so fast away from us, I was hurt. Really hurt. We loved you!"

"What was there for me to stay for? Clean houses like Nellie? Get rough hands and chapped feet. No thanks! I ran away as soon as could. I'm glad I did. I had pretty clothing and men lined up for my favors."

"You were so pretty then," growled Jim.

"Good, I'll bring in my stuff. They just threw it out of the whorehouse. I thought they would understand. But they just got rid of me. Guess I'll have to stand in the street to get business as soon as this kid gets to come." cried Louise as she wiped her eyes.

Louise brought in a bottle of whiskey and stayed drunk until the baby was born. She looked like a hag. There was no luster left in Louise's face or body. Her body looked like a lump of clay. Her face was blotched and resembled a torn paper. As she lay on the floor giving birth to the baby, her life slipped away. She did not fight it, as she was lost.

And so the baby was born, on the floor in a one room shack. Louise left the baby crying as her soul fled her body. She wanted nothing to do with the baby and she was eternally grateful that the Lord took her. Louise entered the Kingdom of Heaven as the baby was born, naked and alone.

Nellie came over and looked at the baby. "Why she looks like whipped cream with a little chocolate whipped in. All toasty mixed white. This girl will be a looker like her mother was, except she is light skinned. What are we going to do with her?"

Jim looked at the little baby laying on his bed. He knew his heart jumped as he looked at her. She was so pretty. It was a shame to be that pretty. What would she do? Would she be like her mother and leave?

"Name her after my mother Clair, except we'll call her Clairese, because she is so little and pretty." said Nellie. "Guess you need to bring her up. Somehow I think you can do it."

"I don't have food even for myself, except what you bring," whispered Jim

"I'll bring more for the baby," said Nellie. "When she is older, I'll take her with me to clean houses. She will be brought up proper, not like Louise. Never did know what was the matter with Louise."

Jim just sat on the bed and stared at the baby. He didn't have much to do, so taking care of the baby was something. He could do it. And if Nellie would take the baby when she was older, than he could live with that. The baby cried and wanted to be fed, but they had nothing to feed her with.

"She needs milk. What are we going to do?" asked Jim

"Don't worry, I'll go get some now. Then you can feed her. I can get bottles from the rich folks. They'll never miss them." said Nellie "I'll get her some sort of clothing. She can't be naked all the time."

So Clairese grew up, wearing left over clothing that nobody wanted. She thrived. She was a good baby. She slept the night away right from the first. She knew she had to be good to exist.

The time came, when Jim was very sick. He lay in the bed and he did not want anything at all except maybe a little water. Clairese loved Jim.

"Come on Grandpa" whispered Clairese, "you have to eat something. Look Grand mother brought you come meat. Can you imagine meat!"

Jim tried to smile at little Clairese. He had learned to love her with a fierce passion. "I'm just not hungry, girl."

Clairese sat on the side of the bed with him. She adored him with her whole heart. He was so good to her. "Just nibble a little meat."

"Can't girl," gasped Jim. "I rather die than eat right now. In fact I might be dying right now. Go fetch Nellie, your grandmother."

"I can't leave you, Grandpa. I just can't," cried Clairese

"Go. You go fetch Grandmother Nellie now. Hurry. You hear me. I just have a little life left to give you over to her forever."

Clairese with her slumped shoulders left the one room house. She cried all the way to Grandmother Nellie's work place. When Grandmother Nellie saw her, she knew that something was wrong. Very wrong!

"Child, where is Jim? Something happen to him? Why are you crying? What is wrong?" shouted Nellie

Nellie held a mop in her strong hands. She looked like she was about to fly away on the mop She dropped the mop and walked over to Clairese. She shook Clairese shoulders. "Stop crying now, you hear."

"Grandpa said you better come now," said Clairese.

Nellie picked up all the supplies that lay around her and bundled them together and put them in the store room. She looked around her and saw she had picked up every thing there was. She turned to Clairese and nodded her head. "Let's go see Grandpa."

They walked over to the shanty town where all the houses were made of discarded wood or paper. Nellie slumped into her body. She knew Jim was not long for this world.

Jim lay in a knot in his bed. The thin cover lay on the floor. Jim looked at Nellie.

"The time has come. I'm not long for this world. I be glad to go. I hated living and I'm scared of dying. If it wasn't for Clairese my life would be a waste. Thank the Lord for the little one. But Nellie, she's all yours now. I am not long for this world."

Jim gurgled or tried to catch his breath, but only his face turned red and as he gasped for air, the life force left him. He lay still in the old bed. Clairese could not believe he had left her. He had been with her since she was born. Here she was five years old and Jim, her Grandpa had left her alone. She knew in her heart of hearts that now she was to work and help Nellie, her Grandma clean houses. She was a house maid and she better be good, or Nellie would throw her out.

Clairese went to live with Nellie and her man, Tom. Her man hated Clairese from the first time he saw her. But Nellie said she would help her clean the houses and so Clairese got o stay. Nellie loved Tom her man, and would do anything for him. He did not work, and all Nellie's money went to him for liquor and drugs. But Nellie adored him, and she worked hard to please him, even if he had a dozen girls on the side.

So at five years old, Clairese went with Nellie to clean the houses of the rich. She polished the tables and cleaned the floors. She was a hard worker. She didn't play with other little children because she was taught to obey and clean. Playing was for the few rich folks, not for the likes of her.

The years flew by, and Clairese came into her beauty. She was eighteen years old and people stopped to stare at her. She was beautiful. Her hair spread around her shoulders and she had a merry laugh. She enjoyed every thing she did. Nellie was old, and could hardly clean a house, but people kept her on as Clairese cleaned with the best of them.

One day, they were cleaning LaCount's house when LaCount came home unexpectedly. He saw Clairese and stopped. She was bent over a table. She lifted her face to the sun. He held his breath. He was about to get rid of his present mistress, and he didn't know if he would kill her or have her have an accident. He made up his mind, killing his old mistress was the best way. He was sure she was dead and no bother to him. He was ready for a new mistress.

He watched Clairese. His breath stopped as he looked at Clairese. She was so beautiful. He watched her as she laughed her merry laughter. She stood up from her cleaning task and he noted her small breasts. He could taste them as he watched her. His cock went hard. He just never had a girl this young, and yet, she was so breathtakingly beautiful.

"Where's your ma?" asked LaCount

Clairese looked up and saw him. He was quality, she could tell just by what he was wearing. "Don't have a ma or pa. Lost my grand father years ago. Only have my grandmother, Nellie"

LaCount was not use to people looking at him the way Clairese was with her big eyes. "Where is she?"

Clairese lowered her head. She knew she was suppose to know her place. "Grandmother Nellie is in the kitchen." Clairese said this under duress. She knew her grandmother was drinking coffee in the kitchen. She would be fired and what would they do? Grandmother Nellie was too old for this work.

LaCount turned around and left the room. He stormed into the hallway that led to the kitchen. He strode straight and tall as he knew who he was. He was the man who ruled New Orleans.

He entered the kitchen, it was just as he thought. The lazy bitch of the old black lady was drinking his coffee. He looked at her as she glanced up. Her face turned almost white with the heat of her thoughts. She knew she was finished here. It was such a good job, and paid so well.

LaCount just stared at her. She got up from her chair and tried to say something that would stop his firing her, but she could think of nothing to say. She knew it was over.

He looked at the rags that Nellie was wearing. He thought of the girl he had seen in the other room; she was in rags also.

He would dress her in velvets and satins. He would put jewels at her throat and hair. He could picture it.

LaCount in his haughty voice said, "I'll give you one hundred dollars for her."

Nellie closed her eyes. She could live on one hundred dollars forever. But to sell her grand daughter? No! She could not do it. She had to think. What were they to do when they lost this job?

LaCount was use to people jumping up on his word. He was not use to someone looking like Nellie. She looked like she didn't know what to do. "O.K. I'll give you one hundred and twenty-five dollars. That is my last offer."

Nellie knew she was going to take the offer. She had to tell Clairese about her being a Mistress. It was far better to be a mistress than a whore. She had to accept. "It's a deal. I'll explain it to Clairese."

Nellie dreaded telling Clairese that she was to be LaCount's mistress. Nellie walked into the room Clairese was cleaning. "Girl, you are lucky. LaCount wants for you to be his mistress. You will wear silks and satins. You will not have to clean houses anymore. You lucky. You hear me?"

Clairese looked at her grandmother Nellie. She could not believe what she was hearing. "Grandma, what are you talking about?"

Nellie shook her head. She had to make Clairese see reason. They could not keep cleaning houses, when they were fired. She could use the money. She would find a place to stay. Her man had left her long ago, and she just had Clairese and herself.

"It's the break we were looking for, you get to wear pretty things, and you get to stay in a nice house. You are lucky." said Nellie slowly

"Leave you?" cried Clairese.

"It's time. I'm old. I can't help you anymore. You need someone to protect you." Nellie said as she leaned her thin body against the door.

Clairese never doubted her grandma's word. It was law. She faced her grandma and spoke softly. "If you think I should then I will, grandma. I always do as you tell."

LaCount came into the room and gave Nellie one hundred and twenty-five dollars in crisp bills. Nellie could not believe that she held so much money in her hands.

LaCount looked at Clairese. "Come along girl. We have things to do. I hate wasted motion."

Clairese went to were LaCount stood and followed him out the door. She followed him up to the bedroom. She did not know what he wanted, but Nellie had said to obey him and she would.

LaCount stood in the most beautiful bedroom that Clairese ever seen. The bed was large and covered in light purple satin. The pillows on the bed were colors of the rainbow, blue and green and red, and purple. There was a large wardrobe and tables with fancy statues. The chairs in the room were all velvet and colored to match the spread.

Clairese gasped in awe. She never seen anything like this before. She only cleaned the downstairs, not the top floors. This was like a miracle.

"There's a bathtub in the other room. Use lots of hot water and scrub yourself clean. I will wait here till you get the dirt off of you and the bugs." said LaCount as he sneered at Clairese.

Clairese had never seen a bathtub before. She was shaken. She did not know what to do. She walked into the little room and saw a tub. It had two knobs. She turned one and hot water ran off her hands. She shut it down. Then she tried the other and cold water ran off her hands. She turned around and saw LaCount looking at her. She felt foolish.

LaCount walked over and turned both knobs. "Get out of your clothing. Now!"

Slowly, Clairese took off the ragged clothing she wore. She stood naked. She watched him looking at her. It was like being eaten alive.

LaCount devoured her. She had just blooming breast. A waist that would be spanned by one large finger, and long, long legs. She was skinny, but he would make her eat some good food. "Get in the water and dunk your hair. I hate bugs."

Clairese put her one foot into the water and felt hot surge through her body. She had never seen a bath, in fact she never even cleaned herself up all the way. She put the other foot in and then slumped down into the tub. She ducked her head into the water and the warm water embraced her. It was such luxury that she never felt like this before.

LaCount walked over to the tub and removed his coat and shirt. He picked up a bar of soap and a wash cloth. "I shall wash you. You are pathetic. It's a wonder I noticed you. You are lucky. I just may keep you."

LaCount bent down and washed Clarisse's hair and her body. He rubbed her tender breast several times. Then he pulled her from the bath and wrapped a big white towel around her body. He smiled to himself. He was going to have a great time.

He laid her on the bed. Then he undressed taking off his boots and his trousers. He stood naked in front of her. Clairese closed her eyes. She never seen a naked man before.

"Open your eyes. Feast on me. I am your lord and master. You will be wise to follow what I tell you." said LaCount as he lay down next to Clairese and the big white towel.

He pulled the towel away from Clairese. He looked at her like one looks at ice cream. Ready to eat! "I will keep you. I never seen anyone as pretty as you. And you are so young. Where have been hiding?"

He stroked her breasts and then he started to suckle them His penis became hard and he hardly controlled himself with his heat. She knew he was sucking her breasts and she did not know what she should do. She just let him do as he wanted. That is what her grand ma had said. Let him do as he wanted.

His fingers roamed into her private parts that were thinly

coated with hair. She was still growing. She thought she would go wild with the touch. He slid into her and could feel the shield that protected her. He was her first man. He was proud of that He loved being first.

He pounded into her and pounded. He could not stop his release. This was so wonderful that he kept pounding on her until he saw her eyes gloss over. He came and he knew the wonders of sex finally. He shook her.

"You are mine now," he said as she looked into her eyes. "Mine to do with as I will."

Later, after the dressmaker came, Clairese put on the dress that was made for her. It was red velvet, low cut, with half her bosom exposed. She put on the jewels, around her wrists, on her neck, on her ears and in her hair. Then she looked into the mirror that was full length. Her eyes widened into round balls. She could not believe what she saw. She saw a queen. A real live queen stared back a her.

"This is quality," she said as she stared into the mirror. "This is a tale of wonder."

She walked sedately out the door and saw the carved stair rail. She put her hands on the wood and stately walked down the steps. She saw LaCount come out the door and stare at her. She smiled. She was so happy, she could not believe it was real. When she came to the end of the stairs, LaCount put out his hand to her and she took it gratefully. It was the beginning of her life.

Clairese wore satins and velvets. She had jewels that covered her neck, her wrists, and her hair. People obeyed every thing she asked for, or her every wish. A queen could not have better subjects. She was held in royal respect. She did not know how wonderful it felt to be the center of attention. She who wore rags and cleaned houses.

Clairese was his choice until she was twenty three years old. She was use to the finer things of life and she expected them as LaCount's mistress. But she heard via the grape vine that he found a new love. He was going to get rid of her. That was when she decided to have her mother become alive once more and she went north to find a hit man. Some one that would kill LaCount without hesitation.

Clairese could not give up the luxury she was use to now. She knew he was going to kill her. He left no loose ends to entangle his life. He was tired of her, and she had given him her life, her blood and her soul. Most of all, she loved the life she lived. It is hard to give up a dream.

Chapter XI

McGuire and Clairese stopped at the front of the wooden house. They had made good time getting to New Orleans. McGuire looked up at his window which was dark.

"Though you won't fit into anything of Helen's, she is so much smaller than you, still you might find something to wear so you look more like a woman. Come along and I will change my clothing so I look more like myself." said McGuire.

Clarisse got off her horse and tied its reigns to the horse post in front of the house. She looked up at McGuire and thought 'No, no, it is Brad, I must remember and cherish each second with him.'

"You sure you want me to go with you, as you talk to Helen?" asked Clarisse.

"Of course," laughed McGuire, "we're family now. Remember?"

Clarisse nodded her head and stood next to the horses they had ridden into New Orleans. "Perhaps I'll just wait till you see Helen and then come up. I'll wait. Sort of in the dark, so people won't notice I'm here."

McGuire bounded up the steps to his door. He ran down the hall to his door, where Helen was suppose to be. He knocked lightly. Nothing happened. He knocked harder. Still just silence. Finally, McGuire yelled, "Helen, Helen, where are you?"

Still silence. McGuire pulled the door open and saw there was nothing there. No clothing, no guns, no Helen. McGuire bounded down the steps to Mrs. Annabelle Smithy's door. He knocked with his fists and his boots. Annabelle Smithy opened the door.

"Oh, No, It's you. I thought you were dead. LaCount said you were dead." Annaebelle stepped back from the doorway.

McGuire looked at Annabelle in her worn dark dress, and bare feet. Her gray hair hung down her back. "Where is Helen?" screamed McGuire. "Where is my sister? She's not in my room. What have you done with her? Did she ever come here?"

McGuire stepped closer; to Annabelle. His hands fisted at his sides. "Answer me, did Helen ever even come here?"

"Why should I tell you. You're a dead man. Leave me alone." shouted Annabelle

McGuire pulled her closer to him with his strong arms. He shook her, "Was Helen even here?"

"Of course she was here. LaCount brought her to me. LaCount said to give her a room without board. That is exactly what I did." exclaimed Annabelle as her finger ran briefly through her knotted hair.

"What has LaCount got to do with Helen?" McGuire dug his fingers into her pudgy arms. "Why would he bring her here?"

"Get your hands off me, you were suppose to be dead. LaCount even said I could sell your things and keep the money. I even have your guns. Silver guns yet. Well they are mine." cried Annabelle as she tugged away from McGuire and was about to close the door in his face.

McGuire pushed the door open. He stepped close to Annabelle. "You better explain and explain very quickly. I am losing my temper and I think I will choke you. I will burn you in oil. First where is Helen, second, I want my guns and ammunition. so you better start explaining."

Annabelle motioned for him to come into her room. She pointed to her dresser where the silver guns lay in their holster and the ammunition next to them. "Didn't have time to sell them yet." she muttered. "I never have luck. Knew I should sell them quickly."

"Helen, where is Helen?" screamed McGuire as he stepped towards her again.

"Oh for heaven sake, sit down, and I'll tell you. No need for you to be so mulish. You should be happy that Helen will be the richest woman in the world. LaCount will drape her in diamonds and who knows what else?"

McGuire walked to the dresser and put his holster on and slipped the guns into the holster. He put the ammunition in his pocket. He sat down on the one skinny chair in the room. "This had better be good. What has LaCount got to do with Helen? All I want to know is where is Helen?"

Annabelle shook her head and took out a cheroot and lighted it. "Well, you should have been here. That's all I can say. Helen and LaCount had an engagement party just days ago. She wore a dress the color of her eyes with a silver lace over it, covered with diamonds. I mean real diamonds. She had a diamond broach in her hair, and around her neck glittered hundreds of diamonds. She had on the earrings of diamonds that touched her shoulders. My it was pretty. And LaCount gave her a diamond ring as big as an apple. My it shone--"

"Helen engaged to LaCount. Impossible. He's, he's, well he's black. Helen would have nothing to do with a black man."

"That may be, but they were together. She as white as paper, and him just as shiny black mahogany. They sure stood out as he announced their engagement."

McGuire stood up. "Announced their engagement? What did Helen do? What did she say?"

Annabelle twisted her fingers together as she watched McGuire pace. "Why she did nothing. She stood there like she was in another world. Guess all those diamonds made her feel special. She just stared and stared. Then he kissed her, and he put her arms around his neck. She just was like a, well, a--"

"For gods sake woman, was she drugged? Where is she now?" screamed McGuire

"Why, they are at the Catholic Church getting married right now. They only had a days engagement. LaCount said he needed a hostess -"

McGuire dragged her body near to his. "Which Catholic church. Tell me now and fast. No more stories, nothing, just which church?"

"The one by the river" "An there was another man looking for her, sort of had-": Annabelle said.

He pulled his hands away from her and he raced to the door. "Lord help you if they are married already. I'll kill you. Do you hear me?" cried McGuire "I knew Helen looked dead by her eyes. She don't care what happened to her. I should never have left her alone. Oh God, It is my fault what ever happens now."

He ran out the door. "Quickly, Clarisse, we got to get to the church. Helen is going to marry LaCount. I can't believe this. I should never have let her come home. But then, she just said she was on her way. Nothing I could really do to stop her."

Clarisse watched as McGuire jumped on his tired horse and pulled Clarisse up to the saddle. Down they went to the old quarter that was LaCount's territory. They noted the iron railings around the top of each building. They knew each house had an inside garden with rooms around the garden. It was not what interested them at the moment. They saw the steeple of the church. It was like the hand of God reaching into the sky.

McGuire could not help thinking that Helen must have

lost her mind to marry a black man. A man like LaCount.
Why he was no good, a devil, a man to fear. He was getting
back at him, McGuire more than he could admit. He should
never have had words with him. McGuire could kick himself
for starting this feud. Maybe, but then again, he sent armed
men to kill him and Clairese. Maybe, just maybe, he really
wanted Helen. He wanted Helen as she was the perfect hostess.
She was beautiful and young, She was graceful. Could he be in
love with Helen. No, that was impossible. He had no heart.

Clairese looked at McGuire. She shivered like someone
was walking over her grave. She was never going to have
happiness. She just felt it. Now LaCount had Helen. And
LaCount wanted to kill her. He kept everything hidden that
he possibly could. What did she know about him. That he had
other mistresses. That he gambled. That he owned half of New
Orleans. That he was not a man to cross as she had, by getting
someone to kill him. He probably found that out and that
was why he was trying to kill her. There was no justice in this
world. She was going to pay for something she had no control
over. But she would never leave McGuire. No, she loved him.
She would do anything for him. Anything. God help her, she
never had loved anyone in her life, and there was nothing she
could do, but keep loving him.

They got off their horses and did not bother to tie them up.
They both rushed inside the church. And bright candle lights
hit their eyes as they came through the doorway. They were
blinded for a second.

Chapter XII

THE BRIGHT LIGHTS HIT McGUIRE and he closed his eyes. When he opened his eyes, he saw the whole church was filled with people. Black and white people sat in row upon row. He never seen so many people together of so mixed in colors. They were all dressed in their fanciest clothing. The colors sang a happy song.

His eyes marched down the aisle. His eyes stopped as he looked at Helen, his sister was here. Then he looked closer and his head became a red blur. LaCounts hand was around Helen's waist. She stood like a manikin, so still and white. She wore a dress of white silk organza that was stewed with real pearls covering most of the dress. Her veil was lace and it also boasted real pearls scattered here and there. Helen's golden hair cascaded down her back in heavy waves which she always wore swept back. The black hand of LaCount stood out in contrast to the white of the dress and Helen's completion.

The Priest was dressed in stark black, with a white band around his neck. He looked up as McGuire and Clairese entered the church. For just a second there was complete silence. The Priest shook his head and continued reading from the Bible.

"Stop," yelled McGuire, "stop right now. Helen is not going to marry you or any one here. You had your revenge for what I did, but let her go."

LaCount turned towards McGuire. "This is not revenge, my friend. Not that I want you near me. This is because I love Helen. I will have her as my wife. Do you doubt it? Ask Helen. She'll tell you, that she will be my wife."

"Never, you black gangster. She will never tie in with you. What do you think I am a fool. You have doped her."

LaCount laughed. "I did not dope her. She is here because she will do as I say, and do what I want. She is mine, and nothing in this world will change that.".

McGuire ran down the aisle. He tried to pulled Helen away from LaCount.

Helen folded over into a dead faint. LaCount held her with both his hands. "What have you done to Helen? You are her brother and you made her faint. Note it was not I who made her faint, but you. "

"I'll never let you marry my sister," yelled McGuire. "We have hated each other for years. You will not wed my sister. Over my dead body will you wed her."

LaCount looked away from McGuire and sharply looked at the priest. "Continue the ceremony. It is almost done."

The Priest looked at LaCount. "But she has fainted."

LaCount closed his hands into fists. "Continue, continue, I say."

The priest stared with his mouth open. He did not want to be involved in this fight. He could tell that there would be pistols drawn and bullets flying. He was a peace loving man, and did not want to be included in this dispute

LaCount turned to McGuire, "Go,"

"Are you crazy and leave you with my sister?" Screamed McGuire

"Get out of here, She is mine, always, always. Even she knows that. She is no longer a virgin. Did you know that? She gave herself to me. Me." snarled LaCount "For all you know she is with my child."

McGuire put his hands on his guns.

LaCount drew out his gun from his jacket. Holding Helen with one hand, he said in a very soft voice, "Go, go now. It is no concern of yours.".

Clairese ran down the aisle. The Indian clothes she wore did not do her justice. They made her look bulky and fat, while in fact she was thin and trim. "Stop this, both of you."

At that instant, LaCount moved his Pistol to point at McQuire's chest. He pulled the trigger, but Clairese threw herself in front of McGuire. The bullet pierced her heart.

The red blood flowed from her chest. McGuire put out his hand and brought her to his chest. The blood covered his shirt. Tears flowed from McQuire's eyes.

"Oh, Clairese, no. No. I love you. Don't die on me." Swifter than a striking snake, McGuire pulled out his silver gun. Slow deliberate aim, and McGuire aimed his gun at his sister. LaCount watched McGuire and his gun. He pulled Helen in back of him.

He said "I love you Helen. I will never let anyone hurt you. You must remember that always. Your brother has lost his mind."

McGuire could not stop his finger from its final position. He shot straight into the heart of LaCount With his last breath on earth, LaCount whispered "I hove you Helen. I shall always love you"

Helen turned around and saw LaCount fall to the floor. She shook her head. It could not be. "LaCount" she screamed.

No answer. Than she looked at her brother. "You meant to shot me. Your sister! Why? Why did you want to kill me?"

"You are not my sister if you marry LaCount. He is a dirty sniveling man of power. You will never live with him. You hear me?" McGuire cried out loudly.

"You were going to kill me?" asked Helen as she looked at Brad McGuire her brother. "You were going to kill me! You really hated Louis LaCount."

"I hated him with all my heart. He was not going to shame

me by marrying you. I would have killed you with pride. I am use to killing people." stated McGuire.

"Look, his blood is like ours. He is like us except he has black skin. You would kill me because he is black?" asked Helen her eyes were glazed. Nothing she saw at the moment. All she noticed was her shock at her brother, and the loss of LaCount.

"No," exclaimed McGuire. "Because I hated him. He was getting even with me. He hated me as much as I hated him. Black don't matter, I was going to wed Clairese."

Helen slumped to the floor. The red blood oozed up her white dress. She did not look. Then she noticed that her brother Brad McGuire was holding Clairese close to his chest. The red blood covered his shirt. Helen just held the head of LaCount to her breast. She could not comprehend anything at the moment. She was in shock.

Her brother, Brad, held Clairese next to his heart. "Clairese, be alive, we have plans." cried McGuire "We are going to have a horse farm, and be married. I love you. You can't be dead. Not again will I lose someone I love."

Helen's veil slipped from her head to the floor. The blood of Clairese and LaCount mingled on the floor. The white veil took the blood as it changed from white to red in color. It became red, deep, dark, red. Helen rocked with LaCount at her breast. Her eyes looked inward. She had not desire to live.

"My God," cried Helen. "His blood is the color of mine. I might be carrying his child. What a mess. What am I to do? You have ruined my life. You Brad, did this to me. All because you hated LaCount. Maybe I did love him. I do not know for sure anymore about who I love and who I hate. But Brad, I can not forgive you for the life you have destroyed. For the life you would have taken, mine!"

McGuire placed Clairese on a seat near where he stood. The people moved over so he could place her. He looked at the crumpled body of LaCount. The man seemed to shrink. Helen stood up looking down on the man. She hardly believed what she saw. She raised her eyes. Her eyes strained. She was going insane. She had illusions of yesterday. She could not help herself, but she shook her head to be rid of the thing she thought she saw.

"Edward's mother," said Helen. "Naturally, you come to see my down fall. You with your clean brown suit, no blood. No nothing. You hated me. Always have. I know your are not real. You are an illusion. Always there, but never there. Have you seen enough? How you must laugh. Helen so very lost. You who busted my life with glee."

The red blood flowed from LaCount and covered the white dress that Helen wore. Helen stood still with the sounds of the guns ringing in the church. She watched the red blood like ink drip across her dress. Her eyes were wide and she seemed to awake from her dreamlike state.

"LaCount," she cried, "LaCount," She bent down to touch his throat. She felt no pulse. She screamed and screamed. Her body shook like a leaf in the wind. Her hands gripped together and then flung out.

McGuire dropped Clairese in a seat and put his arms around Helen. "Hush, baby, it will be all right. Hush," he soothed. "You are safe now. There is no longer the huge man who hated me so much he was going to marry you."

"He loved me. He gave up his life for me. He actually loved me. I did not see it at first, but now I know. He loved me with all his heart and soul."

Helen started into Brad's eyes. Her eyes were wild and they seemed to search for an anchor. "My life, my life, " she cried. "You were going to kill me, and now you tell me to hush?"

"I was going to save you from LaCount. It was the only way I could think of. Oh, Helen, I do love you, but you could never marry LaCount. I hate him. I hated him."

McGuire hugged her tightly. She stopped screaming and

the tears ran down her face. "I may have his baby. I may have his baby." she cried. "Do you realize what you have done? There will be no father. No one to love him. I am lost. You who hated him so were ready to kill, and without a conscience. You would have killed me."

"Oh, God, no,"

She buried her head in McGuire's shoulder. The tiredness seemed to grip her. Her blonde hair was streaked with blood. She seemed like a lost child. The blood dripped off her dress. She stared at her veil that lay on the floor. Covered with blood it looked like a rag.

"I don't know what to do?" she cried. "I don't know what will be."

Brad watched her with a blank stare. He did not know why he would want to kill his sister, his only kin.

People in the pews started to stir. At first they sat still watching the drama around them. The display of hatred and of love. The blood that stained the floor. Then they looked at the Priest. The priest stood very still. He had never seen blood in the church before. The body of Christ was looking below at this violence. What was happening here, thought the Priest? The people moved their bodies in a slow wave like motion. They did not want to attract attention to anyone who wore a gun. They hardly dared think about what they had witnessed. They started to slip out of the church silently. Slowly, the church became empty except for Brad and Helen, and the dead bodies no one was left. The Priest stood like stone as he did not know what to do. He watched the people leaving the church and did not stop them. He was devastated over the blood that washed the wooden floor. He came for a wedding, that turned into a blood bath.

LaCount ran the whole of New Orleans and some how they would blame him. His death left a void on who would take over. Someone had to lead the way that New Orleans would be run. Someone with power. Would they blame him?

No! They would take control, and make believe that this never happened. He was blameless.

In the stillness of the church a loud cry came suddenly. "Helen, Helen." was heard.

Helen pushed back from her brother. She felt like she faced the past. She could feel her heart start to beat. It was like it was breathing and living again. But it could not be. She was not living in the world of what could not be, as the past had left her alone and broken. Her glazed eyes started to tear. She was a lost soul.

Helen stood up and looked around as if she world had stopped. It had. She saw Edward. Could it really be Edward, or surely, she has lost her mind. How could Edward be here in New Orleans. She had seen his mother, but that was a ghost of the past. Now she glimpsed Edward. She wanted to sink into the bloody floor.

Edward's hair so like white gold was gilded by the stained glass windows. He was an angel in disguise. Helen exclaimed to herself that she was going mad. He strode down the aisle of the church. His hand were out ready to catch Helen.

He put his hands around Helen's waist. "Helen,"

She looked up at him. Surely she had lost her mind. Edward, her Edward in New Orleans. Impossible! He was in London, doing whatever Dukes do.

Helen raised her face up. Edward lowered his face and kissed her full on the lips. He moaned as he held her. Then he kissed her again, but this time as one would kiss his love, his life.

Slowly, faintly, Helen whispered, "Edward?"

"Helen, oh, Helen," cried Edward. "I cannot live without you."

"Am I mad? Can it really be you?" cried Helen. "You can not be real. You are a Duke. Duke's do not come to New Orleans. Duke's must live as dukes do. Or Whatever."

"I hired a private investigator to find you. I did not know

where to find you. The moment he gave his report, mother and I caught the first ship going this way. I can not live without you. I left London and came as fast as I could to marry you," said Edward. "I can never love anyone else. Helen, I love you. I am here. I can not live without you."

"Your mother-" cried Helen. "I swear I saw her. It is a dream. It can't be real."

"She came also. I told her I would never marry anyone but you. She came to her senses. She knew I meant it. Helen, I love you." said Edward.

He pulled her close to his body. She became overwhelmed with his strong body, his smell of tobacco and leather. Helen's senses whirled. She wanted to die right there and be happy that she lived long enough to dream Edward here in the Church.

She shuttered as she looked at Edward. Blood and guts, love and laughter, yes, she was going mad.

He held Helen closely to his chest. Their bodies melded into one. The blood that was on Helen's dress now covered Edwards white jacket. His ascot was bright red as the blood, and his shirt was a soft light gray also covered with blood.

"I am happy now." said Helen in a low whisper. "I can dream Edward is here, and I am in his arms. Nothing matters to me now. LaCount is dead, and I may be carrying his child. Does it matter now?"

Helen dug deeper into Edwards chest. Her arms went around his neck. Her face was hidden in the folds of his jacket. "Oh, love, oh, love," she cried. "This moment of madness is the best that can be. I shall die happily."

"Helen, you shall now never get away from me again. We shall marry right now. The priest is here and this is a church." Edward stated "I have waited long enough to tell you I love you, and only you." Edward pulled her away and looked into her eyes. Deeply into her sky blue eyes. He noted the glazed and dazed emotion that her eyes held.

Helen stared at him. "I can not marry you. I may have

LaCount's child. I do not know. I am not the same girl you knew. I am doomed forever. Why do I still dream of you? Why are you always in my thoughts? Do you know, LaCount did love me. He was so strong at times. Did I love him? I do not know what to think."

"Helen," Edward said in the soothing voice, "you can blame my mother, or what ever you want. You can have twenty children from other fathers, it does not matter to me. I want you. I want you to marry me now, before anything else happens. I want to marry you before God, and know that you shall always be mine. If you are pregnant, I shall make the child mine. But you can not run away again. I love you, I love you."

"You are real? You are real?" Helen asked as she looked into Edward's eyes. "I may be pregnant with a black child. I can never give up a child. It is mine. Do you understand?" Her eyes focused on Edward.

"It is truly you," said Helen as she sniffed his clothing. "I thought I would never see you again. Why are you here? What brought you to the New World? And what about your mother. Your mother who hates me with all her heart."

"Helen, I do not want you to give up the child. I want you, anyway I can get you. Can you understand the anguish I have gone through to find you. I can not ever let you go again." Edward said as he pulled Helen closer. Their bodies melded and the blood ran freely down their sides.

Helen looked down at the dead bodies that lay near her feet. She wanted to throw up, to end her life now. "Edward, I love you enough to know I can never marry you. I am not right for you, especially now. Look around at the flood of blood all around us. How can you think of marriage or for that matter, anything but death?"

"Because my dear, I have traveled far and wide to find you again. Do you think that I will let you go again. You are my life and my love." said Edward

"How can I marry, covered in blood?" cried Helen

"It is no use to worry over blood. We need to marry to be sure that we are together forever. Do you understand? Look at me. I want you. I will have you. I do not worry about your not being a virgin. It was my mother's fault but just as much, my fault. This should never have happened. I should never have let you go. Please, Helen, marry me now."

Helen stared at the blood on her dress. It crept up like a river of red ink. She looked at her brother, Brad. His eyes were wet with tears as he bent over Clairese.

"I loved her," McGuire whispered "What is wrong with me? Why do women I love leave me always alone? We were going to Texas to start a horse farm. We were to be married."

"Brad," Helen called, "what shall I do? You who pointed a gun at me and was going to kill me? Should I believe that Edward really wants me? Should I trust my heart?"

Brad McGuire looked at his sister. "Take what happiness you can, love, too soon it is ripped away from you. Do you love Edward?

"With all my heart," cried Helen

"Then marry him now, here and now. It is right, forget the blood and guts, Do it now and forever be thankful you had the opportunity to have love." said McGuire. "I lost my love. I was so sure that I had found what I was looking for. What a fool I was. Nothing is as planned or thought to be. First it was Samantha, I thought I would never live again. Then, I fell in love with Clairese. She who is dead at my feet. I shall never have happiness."

Edward took Helen's hand. He turned to the priest. "Marry us now. Listen to me, and stop standing there like stone. Marry us."

The priest shook his head. He looked at the dead bodies that were laying on the floor. He looked at the blood that seemed to spread in every direction. Then he looked at Edward, and he saw raw emotion. He imagined he saw his death, if he did not do his bidding. He picked up his Bible that had fallen to the floor. He looked at the pages that were covered with blood. He then looked at Helen and shook as he saw the red blood blowing still over her dress.

"Perhaps we should clean up and change," said the Priest. "It might be better."

"No," said Edward very slowly. "Now, while we are here and you are here. This is a matter that must be settled now. I love Helen. I want to marry her. I want to marry her here and now."

Helen shook her head. "Edward, I need to change my dress. We need to clean up this mess. Brad is feeling so terrible. We have to wait."

"No," cried Edward, "I have waited long enough. Do you understand?"

'Edward, what can I say, I can not marry you with blood and bodies all around on the floor of the church. I can not marry you in fairness because I am not a virgin any more. I have to give you up."

Edward pulled Helen into his arms. He kissed her with passion and longing. "I know this is terrible. But it will be worse with my mother here. We have such little time. Do you think I do not know my mother is looking at us right now. It is now, and now we shall marry."

Edward spoke to the priest. "Marry us right now."

The priest nodded and the ceremony began with the bloody book open to the Wedding Ceremony which thankfully the priest knew by heart. There was no reading from the blood stained book. The two bodies lay on the floor, blood flowing on the floor, on Helen's dress and on Edward's attire. McGuire looked at the blood on his shirt. One thing he was sure, this was going to be a bloody marriage, what with Edward's mother and all.

The Priest finished the ceremony. He looked at Edward as if asking permission to leave. The priest intoned "You are married now. Can I leave? This had been a bad day for me. I do not think you want to kiss the bride with all this around. "

Just as he said that, an unholy cry echoes in the church. "Edward, Edward"

Edward just shook his head and said, "That is mother, I told you she was here. She wants to stop our marriage, but it is too late. She waited in the church too long."

"I can't believe we are married. It was my dream," said Helen. "I think I saw your mother before I saw you. She was here. She is real. She was here with all this mess. She knows about LaCount. She knows I might be pregnant. She knows all."

Edwards mother rushed down the aisle of the church. She stopped and stared at the dead bodies laying near the altar. She gasped. Her face turned as pale as ocean foam. "Blood," she cried. "Dead people, oh Edward, what have you done?"

"We are married now, Mother," said Edward. "you waited too long in this church to stop us. You ruined everything I loved, but not this. This is it. I am married and we are going home now."

Helen stared at his mother. She stared at the brown suit that was so clean without any blood. Then she noticed the shoes. The shoes were bloody. She knew that his mother would have stopped the marriage if she wanted to. She had been there all the time. She wanted Edward to be happy. She wasn't so bad. She knew when she was licked.

"Ah mother, it is your doing," said Edward slowly, "If you had not chased Helen away none of this would have happened. I hope that you are satisfied. She would not have been on the river boat. Brad would never have been there to fall in love with Clairese, LaCount would not have fallen in love with Helen, and then there would have been no blood or bodies. It is your miserable butting in that caused all this to happen."

Edward's mother nodded her head. "I did wrong. I should never have butt in. I am sorry for the misery I caused. Please forgive me."

Edward's mother pulled the ribbons on her brown bonnet. She wore a brown cape with mink on the inside, and under that she had on a brown suit of silk with embroidered roses. Her face turned red with anger.

"How dare you blame me for this horrible blood laying on the church floor. I never had anything to do with it. I asked you to forgive me. It is over. I confess I did wrong. " cried Regina, Edward's mother.

"Perhaps, mother, but Helen and I are married. Now what do you have to say?" asked Edward

Pulling a handkerchief from her pocket, Edward's mother started to cry. Great racking sobs came out of her mouth. Edward placed his hands on his mother. "I still love you too." He pulled his mother to his chest and kissed her. "I shall always love you." Edward's mother stopped crying and stared at her baby. She caressed his chin. She put herself together and walked slowly out of the church. She looked at the blood on her shoes, but her crisp suit and cape held no blood. There was nothing she wanted to do about it. It was over.

Edward turned to Helen. "I think we should leave now my dear. Let them clean up the place and all. Get you dressed to travel back to England. The bloody dress is sort of ruined."

Edward smiled and pulled Helen to him. Helen's eyes were dazed. She seemed to think she was some place else. Edward grabbed her and walked out of the church, leaving Brad alone with Clairese.

Brad McGuire walked out of the church. He had lost every thing he loved. He had wanted a new life, but Clairese was dead and he was alone. He looked at Edward's mother. She shriveled where she stood. She looked old.

Edward's mother stood by the door of the church. She thought about what had happened. Then she said to herself, "Do you think that they will talk to me after all I have done?"

Brad was standing near the door and heard Edward's

mother. She looked so sad. He knew she was sorry for what she had done. There was no going back.

"Perhaps if you try they will love you as you deserve. But your best bet would be to repeat that you made a mistake and you are sorry for it. I'll tell you the truth, my sister is a sucker for any one who admits they made a mistake:" said McGuire. "She sure made a mistake by coming here. Now there is nothing to do, but hope for the best."

Edward's mother fanned herself with her fan, she had taken from her coat pocket. She felt so faint standing by the door of the church. She turned on her heels and walked over to Brad McGuire.

"I have butted in too much. I thought it was for the best. I was wrong. I hope that they will forgive me, in truth, in time. I am just an old busy body. Just to think, England seems so far away. Do you think your sister will have a black baby? Do you think she is pregnant? What will we do?" asked Edward's mother

McGuire looked at her and shook his head. "No sense trying to guess. What will happen. Just remember, it is all because of you the my sister came out this way. All because of you that everything bad happened to us. I just hope you keep out of their lives and let them live it like they want. I can't believe that I was going to kill my own sister. What is rage about? What was I thinking?"

"I have learned my lesson," said Edward's mother. "from now on I say nothing. Yet, I can't believe that Edward and Helen married with all that blood on the floor. The dead not rising to resist. I can not believe it all happened. Well, it is time to go home and face the music. My husband, his sister, Edward and Helen. "

Chapter XIII

BRAD MCGUIRE WATCHED THE RIVER boat leave the dock. He looked at the paddle wheels as they turned the water into a waterfall. He thought of Helen, his sister and all she would be facing. Yet, with Edward at her side, she would make it. No doubt about that. She was a born survivor. So much had happened in their lives. Yet, they would live with it. Cherish it and hold it close to their hearts.

"Well, at least Helen and Edward were married. What a mess of blood and guts in that church. Hope they cleaned it up. I hope that Helen can get along with that mother of Edwards. Boy, she is a hard one to crack. But Helen can sweet talk anyone."

McGuire watched the steam boat as it got smaller and smaller. He felt so alone. He sort of wished Helen was with him, not that he blamed her for marrying Edward. Slowly, he walked back to his apartment, his mind in a torrent.

"I might as well get my stuff and get out of this city. This place is not for me. I quit gambling and all it stands for. I'm off of it forever. I can smell the river from my apartment. I can see the eyes of Clairese watching me. The smell of the river makes me want to cry as I think of Clairese. Oh, I loved her so. Would she know it? She gave up her life to save me. Did she know I loved her?"

He packed his belongings in a carpet bag. He walked out of his apartment. He called a hearty good-by to his land lady. He did not stop to hear if she called back a good-by. His mind was on Clairese and on their plans to move to Texas.

One thing he knew was horses. Yes, living on a plantation did that. He could almost smell a great horse, from a bad one. He was going to start a horse farm. What a laugh. Now that he lost everything he was going to raise horses. But he was not going to go to Texas as he planned with Clairese, he would go to California. He would take his time going across the country. He was sure to rush through Arizona because he did not want to remember. He didn't want to be reminded of LouLou or anything in his past. He was going to start new. He was going to be something his parents wanted him to be. He was going to raise and tame horses. It was time to settle down.

He jumped on his great black horse. Chip. He tied the carpet bag to the back of his saddle. Brad McGuire sat straight in the saddle. He headed West, out of New Orleans. He could not stay in New Orleans, He could not go back to Arizona, nor would he go to Texas with his dreams. His dreams were all dead. Clairese was gone forever.

Only one place left for me, he thought, I'll go to California. Can't go further than that. I can just go and go and go. Whatever does it matter. No one to care what I do now. It is time to just wander.

Brad McGuire sat straight in the saddle. Once again he wore black, black shirt, pants and hat seemed to cry for the dead. His silver guns gleamed in the sun light. He pulled he reins of his black horse and they slowly left New Orleans.

'California, an unknown land, it could not remind him of Samantha, or Clairese. He did not want to remember the bright light that was Clairese, nor the fact that he almost killed his sister, Helen. A new start, a new beginning and a new life. He had to remind himself that he was through with all women.

As he slowly left the town, he did not know what awaited him in California He really had no great expectations. How was he to guess that he would meet the Senorita that would change his life forever.

\#   \#